FAREWELL

A SHORT STORY

Stevie Turner

OTHER BOOKS BY STEVIE TURNER

A HOUSE WITHOUT WINDOWS
A LONG SLEEP
A RATHER UNUSUAL ROMANCE
ALYS IN HUNGERLAND
BARREN
CRUISING DANGER
EXAMINING KITCHEN CUPBOARDS
FALLING
FINDING DAVID: A PARANORMAL SHORT STORY
FOR THE SAKE OF A CHILD
HIS LADYSHIP
LEG-LESS AND CHALAZA
LIFE: 18 SHORT STORIES
LILY: A SHORT STORY
MIND GAMES
NO SEX PLEASE, I'M MENOPAUSAL!
PARTNERS IN TIME
REPENT AT LEISURE
REVENGE
SCAM!
THE DAUGHTER-IN-LAW SYNDROME
THE DONOR
THE NOISE EFFECT
THE PILATES CLASS

TABLE OF CONTENTS

DESCRIPTION 6

Chapter One...7

Chapter Two 13

Chapter Three 17

Chapter Four...23

Chapter Five 29

Chapter Six 33

Chapter Seven...37

Chapter Eight..44

Chapter Nine..48

Chapter Ten 51

Chapter Eleven 55

Chapter Twelve 60

Chapter Thirteen..65

Chapter Fourteen 72

Chapter FifteeN 81

Chapter Sixteen 86

Chapter Seventeen 91

Chapter Eighteen 95

Chapter Nineteen 102

Chapter TWENTY...107

Chapter Twenty ONE..111

Chapter Twenty two 115

DESCRIPTION

Kickback have a problem; their manager Richard has booked a string of sold-out concert venues, but ageing has taken its toll on the band and now they're not sure whether they can manage a long tour anymore. Seth will need steroid injections in order to sing, Rob has prostate trouble, Ethan has RSI and tennis elbow and cannot make his beloved Flying V guitar cry or sing, and years of being hunched over a drum kit has given Mick an arthritic back.

Ethan suggests calling his friend Baz to help play any guitar solos. Baz is willing to help, but has already checked himself into rehab. Baz meets a fellow alcoholic, Steve, in rehab, whom he discovers has more than a passable voice. He suggests bringing Steve along to the rehearsal sessions as a backing singer when both of them have dried out, and the rest of the band agree.

However, once Baz and Steve arrive at Seth's mansion in deepest Wales, a tragic event occurs that none of the band could have ever foreseen and which threatens the commencement of what will now be the band's farewell tour.

CHAPTER ONE

He shifted his head just a fraction to the right to allow rays from the mid-afternoon sun to shine through one of the rooftop's crenellations and flood his face with warmth. A persistent wasp encroached further into his personal space, intent on making another attempt to access dregs from the last can of ice-cold lager left over from lunch. Seth Hurley, languid from Gwyneth's smoked salmon soufflé, raised his upper body off the sun lounger, drank the remains of the lager and followed the wasp with his eyes as he flung the empty can across the flat roof.

"It's all yours, you little bastard."

Naomi, stark naked, lay prostrate next to him. He nudged her soft flesh with his elbow.

"Turn over. You're about done on that side."

"You just want to see my tits, don't you?" Naomi blew a kiss in Seth's direction and heaved herself onto her back. "Happy now?"

"Yeah, the view's good from here."

Even extreme heat and a post-lunch dip could not deter Seth from taking an appreciative view of his wife's body, still toned and supple despite the big 5-0 approaching in a few years' time.

"Full marks to the divine potter."

"Bugger off." Naomi stretched and yawned. "It's too hot for sex."

From a distance, the increasing sound of a helicopter's blades cut through a chorus of birdsong. Seth threw the first thing he could find to cover Naomi's attributes.

"Oh, now you've got my kimono all full of sun cream." Naomi propped herself up. "What did you do *that* for?"

"I think he passed by a while ago. I recognise the markings. If it's a perv, he's not getting another eyeful."

"It might be a female pilot."

"Yeah…well…", Seth hiked the kimono higher over Naomi's shoulders, "*she's* not going to have a look either, especially if she's a lezzo."

"Paparazzi, do you think?"

"Could be." Seth made a *'tut'* of annoyance. "How the hell have they found us so soon? We've only been here a fortnight."

"Gwyneth has probably tittle-tattled to all and sundry in the village, I expect. Who knows *what* they're saying when they jabber away in Welsh? I'm sure the grapevine must have stretched all the way down to London by now."

"No, she's not daft… she'd be in breach of her contract. Let's not get paranoid." Seth shook his head. "I like it here."

"At least you know *I'm* genuine." Naomi turned her head to wink at him. "I fell in love with you all those years ago when you didn't have a pot to piss in."

"And now I've got too many pots. Put your bikini back on… the security guy is wandering about downstairs and Gwyneth doesn't finish 'til three. Let's go down to the gym and the plunge pool, and maybe afterwards we can have a swim outside. At least nobody can see us in the basement."

Seth jumped up and ran for the roof access door, previous languor vanishing in an instant as the helicopter whirred overhead. Naomi panted behind whilst struggling to don bikini bottoms in a hurry. They ran in through the access door then slammed it behind them.

"Bloody hell, if it is the *paps*, they'll do anything for a front page scoop."

"If they knew what I was thinking, then they'd have an even bigger story." Seth began to make his way down the narrow stairs to the fourth floor. "Richard's going to ring again any day now, and I don't think I can face another tour."

Only silence emanated from his wife of twenty five years. Seth reached the fourth floor then turned around to face Naomi.

"For a start, Ethan's got RSI and is still practising other ways to play, and Mick's got back trouble after nearly thirty years behind the drums. Rob's already more than ten years older than the rest of us, who are all pushing fifty. I can't hit the high notes anymore. The band's getting too old for cock-rock. We'll look bloody ridiculous."

Naomi's expression registered complete surprise.

"The Stones are still going, and they're nearly eighty."

"Yeah, but *we've* had enough. There's around four hundred million pounds in the bank, if you count our portfolio of shares as well. Manny's looked after us well. I don't need to do this crap anymore."

"But what else will you do? You'll be crawling the walls within a month. The record company will sue... you're under contract to promote the new album, you *know* you are."

He detected a desperate tone to her voice.

"I'll do a few TV and radio interviews, and the office can send out stuff. I'll pretend I've got industrial pox. I'm done, babe, I've had enough and so have the other guys. If they want to sue, well… I can afford it."

Hand-in-hand, and with Naomi now wearing her bikini and kimono, they padded down the grand staircase in the direction of the gym without speaking, except to nod in passing to Gwyneth as she carried clean laundry upstairs. Seth, glad of the release of pent-up worries, sighed and felt that a great weight had been taken off his shoulders.

The air-conditioned coolness of the basement was a welcome balm to his troubled soul. Seth guided Naomi through the gym and into the small plunge pool area. Free as a bird and safe in the knowledge there would be no more back-breaking tours, he let go of Naomi's hand and flung himself feet first into the pool and enjoyed a brief spell underwater. When at last he came up to the surface, Naomi stood at the edge of the pool.

"Gwyneth's just brought your mobile… Richard's rung, just as you said he would."

His genial mood evaporated. As she spoke he could hear AC/DC's *'It's a Long Way to the Top if you Wanna Rock and Roll'*, Richard's individual ring tone.

"Tell him I'm dead."

"You can't keep putting him off. I'm going to answer it."

"No!" Seth hauled himself out of the pool. "Fucking don't!"

Too late, Naomi had already accepted the call.

"Yes, he's here, Richard. Hold on."

He strode to a nearby lounger and wiped his hands on a towel. Glaring at Naomi, Seth snatched the phone from his wife's hand and put it to his ear.

"What?"

"What d'you mean, *what*? Didn't you get the email? Tour dates for September and October, that's what. Get off your arse and give 'em *what's what*."

"I know we agreed on another tour before we recorded the album, but that was a year ago. Have you spoken to the others?" Seth dabbed his eyes dry. "They're not keen... none of us are."

"They're up for it... they've heard how much they're going to earn. I've been trying for days to get hold of you. Arenas are booked... hello Birmingham, Sheffield, Manchester, Newcastle and Glasgow! Then there's the O Two before finishing at Wembley. Tickets are already sold out, so I've added extra days."

"Fuck." Seth sighed. "I can't do it anymore, Rich."

"You'll have to or we'll be taken to the cleaners. Manny'll have a fit with his legs in the air. Topperman Records will drop you like a hot brick. You *have* to promote the new album, you *know* that. Everybody wants a cut of this one. It's selling like hot cakes."

Seth pressed the red 'exit call' button and flopped down onto the lounger. Almost immediately AC/DC's intro started up again. Lying flat, Seth pressed '*accept*'.

"Can't you just bugger off?"

"No can do. Get practising in that new shit-hot studio of yours. You've got three months to get in shape."

Seth sat up and threw the phone into the pool. Richard's terse voice droned on up to the point when the phone sank beneath the water.

***

He always disliked a camera being shoved up his nose. The feeling was altogether very unpleasant. James Barnard, The Ear, Nose and Throat surgeon, wore a kind of 3D headset, and to Seth seemed lost in the intricacies of the vocal cords on display.

"Count to ten for me."

Seth's voice sounded mightily peculiar as he counted. The numbing spray he'd had to the back of his throat didn't help either.

"Your vocal cords have lost some elasticity and flexibility, and the larynx muscles seem a little thinner and weaker compared to when I last saw you, which is common as we age. We can give you some voice rehabilitation and a little injection of filler if you're willing."

"Well, we haven't toured for five years, and I've been living the good life. *Too* good, I think. It's been easier just singing in the studio, but hey, anything you can do, Jim. I'm counting on you for this upcoming tour."

"I'll do my best. I'll call you in for the filler soon, and then book you in for the rehab. The filler will last a few years before it needs to be done again. I'll go in through the skin in your neck, but you'll need to be awake so I can hear if your voice improves."

"Sounds peachy, and possibly right up there with my root canal surgery. I'm already looking forward to it." Seth sniffed as the camera left his nostril. "I'm still not sure if I *can* do, or even *want* to do, another tour though, but hey…seems I *have* to."

CHAPTER TWO

Ethan Taylor wondered how the hell he could play a bloody note whilst standing bolt upright, when for forty years he had adopted the kind-of-cool low-slung, bent-over posture much favoured by generations of rock guitarists.   However, if he ignored Stretch-it-Out Tony's advice and continued to keep his left wrist bent, numb fingers due to carpal tunnel syndrome would soon ensure he would be unable to play at all.   And there was more; without ever having batted a lob, volley, backhand or forehand, his left arm had also acquired tennis elbow.

Life sucked, and now Richard had emailed the next lot of tour dates.   Ethan grabbed the fretboard, stretched his fingers into some power chords and then a quick run in A minor, and winced as a sharp pain shot through the outside of his elbow.

It was time to break bad news.   Still drumming the fingers of his left hand on the guitar's fretboard, Ethan reached over for his mobile phone and scrolled down his list of contacts until Seth's number appeared.

"Hiya, you arsehole."   Ethan, guitar on chest, laid himself down on his studio sofa. "It's no good.   I've tried, but I'm in too much pain to play.   I've just decided to go with Tony's advice and have the tennis elbow and carpal tunnel ops.   I'll be out of action for a few months, but at least Cindy won't have to wipe my arse for me. Sorry mate, you'll have to see if Baz can do the tour."

"Christ. Not *you* as well?

His friend's voice sounded unusually thin and reedy. Ethan chuckled.

"Sorry, can't be helped. Fancy a pint? Come round and I'll get some beers in."

"I've moved to Wales now, remember?"

"Shit. Heavy night. Mick came over. He was drinking to dull the pain from his back, then he fell sideways off the drum stool. Anyway, he said Rob's got the Old Man disease. D'you want *me* to ring Baz?"

"Rich can sort it. Anyway...*what* Old Man disease? Crabs?"

"His prostate's playing up." Ethan wrapped his left arm around the guitar. "He keeps wanting to piss, but he can't."

"Well, what with my voice going *a*wol... that's just about finished us off then. Rich will *have* to sort us out some interviews instead. Good luck with the ops. See you soon, mate."

"Yeah. Bye for now."

Ethan wrapped both his arms around the guitar and cursed his advancing years.

***

He felt himself being shaken awake.

"I'm sure you love your guitar more than you do *me*. There were three of us in the bed last night. That bloody thing nearly took one of my eyes out."

"I fell asleep playing it." Ethan yawned and sat up. "Of course I love you more, don't be stupid."

But he knew she wasn't *that* stupid; Cindy had already worked it out. Yeah, what did a middle-aged bloke have in common with a woman thirty five years younger? Only one thing, and he wasn't even getting *that* at the moment. If only Rita had found a way to offset the menopause. Ethan rubbed his eyes. No, that didn't matter to him now. He'd have her back tomorrow, complete with the hot flushes, mood swings and lack of sex.

"New top? That's nice."

"You bought it for me six months ago."

"Oh."

He watched Cindy's cute backside as she stomped out of the room. He sighed. Life wasn't working out exactly as he had hoped. Okay, to his dying day he'd never have to worry about money, but could he cope with never being able to step onto a stage again? There was also a huge gap in his life since his divorce from Rita, and so far Cindy had not filled it. He could write twenty love songs about Rita, but it wouldn't ever make her come back to him now that she had a lezzie fiancé. He'd blown it. *Finito.*

Ethan stood up and put his prized Flying V on its stand. No good would come of endlessly trying to find another way to play; there wasn't one. He needed to surgically remove himself from all guitar solos, and come to think of it, from Cindy too. Perhaps the tour would be a good break from her after all. Baz would be able to play the solos if he could manage to stand upright for long enough, and leave *him* free to play rhythm. He could fill himself with painkillers and have the operations after the tour. Yeah ... he needed to set his girlfriend free; she was only twenty years old and had her whole life in front of her. What the hell was he playing at, taking a baby from its cradle? He must have had a male menopause at the same time as Rita's. It was time to take stock of his life, and the first thing that needed doing was to get a proper haircut. The long, grey straggling locks were not a kindness to others; no wonder Rita had divorced him.

CHAPTER THREE

Rob Hughes had tried his best, but there was still nothing to show for half an hour standing at the urinal except for a half-hearted trickle. He sighed. His sixty seventh birthday was only a month away, and now it looked as though he had inherited the same problem as his elderly father, well... thankfully without the cancer. It was time to end the 'watchful waiting' his GP had advised; Finasteride, and then the blast of embolisation beads to cut off some of the prostate's blood supply. This would need to be his 67th birthday present to himself. The gold LaFerrari would have to wait.

"What are you doing in there?"

Maddie's voice cut through his thoughts like a knife. Rob zipped up his fly and washed his hands.

"What the fuck d'you *think* I'm doing?"

The door to the marbled *his and hers* bathroom opened and his wife, glittering in gold lamé but with her hair still in curlers, popped into view.

"We're going to be late for Rita and Danni's engagement party if you don't put those porn mags away."

"Bring me one and I'll have a look at it." Rob wiped his hands on a towel. "It'll be more fun than wasting half an hour I'll never get back again trying to have a piss. Anyway, I don't feel like going to a party... Rita's *your* friend... *you* go."

"Oh, *come on!*" Maddie barged over to her sink and ripped out each curler one by one. "Stop being so miserable. I don't want to walk in there all on my own."

"And I don't want to go to some lesbo gathering. I never liked Rita anyway...*and* I'll be the only bloke there."

"Ethan and Cindy are going. Rita's invited Mick and Sonia as well.

"Yeah? She asked Ethan?" Rob looked with appreciation at Maddie's slender figure. "You never said."

"You never asked."

***

He'd never seen an engagement cake with two would-be brides on it before. Rob grabbed a beer from the Dorchester Hotel's free bar, fondled his wife's buttocks momentarily, and wondered whether or not Ethan cared about how some of his divorce settlement had been spent.

"It's too dangerous giving Mick access to free booze for the night." Rob waved at his band mate who had just entered the function room. "It won't end well. Mark my words."

"I didn't think he'd been invited, but Sonia will keep him under control just as long as she's in-between lovers." Maddie's eyes swept the room. "Oh ... I spoke too soon. Sonia doesn't seem to be with him."

"Why doesn't Mick ever find out?"

"No one dares to tell him. Watch out Rob, he's coming over."

Rob just had enough time to put his beer down on a nearby table. Mick cleared the dance floor in a few strides and stood grinning opposite Rob. Two muscular arms slapped around Rob's back and lifted him clean off the floor.

"Let's liven up these dykes, Rob."

"Mick... no. Put me down." Rob flailed his arms about. "Remember last time?"

"Not really. I was shit-faced." Mick winced and dropped Rob like a hot brick. "Ow, my back's absolutely fucked."

Rob smoothed out creases in his suit. Ethan and Cindy approached them, and Rob pointed a finger at Ethan's hair.

"Where's the ponytail?"

"It fell off." Ethan gave Mick's stomach a playful punch. "I needed to stop looking like a wanker."

"Now you just look *old*." Cindy grabbed Maddie's arm. "Come on, let's go and talk to Rita."

"What's up with *her*?" Rob gave an appreciative glance at Cindy's backless gown as she walked away. "She looks like she's chewed a wasp."

"I told her we needed some time apart. I've decided I'll do the tour if Baz can help me out and do the solos. I just need to get away."

"I've told Rich *I* can't do it." Rob ignored his bursting bladder and finished his pint. "It takes me all day just to have one piss."

"Wear a nappy. Elton John did. He said so in his book." Mick gulped down a pint of beer in one go.

"Yeah, but wasn't he in fancy dress? I'm not going on stage as Donald Duck."

"Look mate, this tour, call it a farewell one if you want, might be the last time we can all play together. Seth can get a shot of steroid or something, *you* can wear a nappy, Baz can help Ethan out as long as he can see straight, and I'll wear a corset if I have to."

"Like Madonna? It won't suit you." Rob roared with laughter. "Cones as well?"

"Of course." Mick lifted his shirt. "See? I've got *moobs*."

"What're you boys plotting over here in the corner?" Rita, arm-in-arm with Danni, walked towards them. "You must be up to *something*, especially Ethan. Mick, put your shirt down."

"We're going to do a farewell tour." Mick tucked his shirt back into his trousers. "I've just decided. Anyone who says no is *dead*."

"Good luck with *that* then." Rita moved closer to Danni. "Danni and I will be in the Bahamas."

"How much will that cost me?" Ethan, face impassive, munched on a vol-au-vent.

"Just the house. Remember the divorce settlement?"

"How could I forget? Me and Cind are down to paper plates now."

"Ignore him, Danni." Rita scowled at Ethan. "Let's carry on mingling. He's already started to wind me up. Good luck with the tour, Mick."

"Let's face it, we're over the hill." Rob shrugged his shoulders as Rita and Danni walked away. "Who's gonna pay to see *us*?"

"People *our* age will, 'cos they're still buying our records." Mick beckoned a waiter. "Three more pints of real ale please, mate." He turned back to Rob and Ethan. "All the fifty and sixty year olds are just gagging to re-live their mis-spent youth and mosh along to *Kickback*."

"You reckon?" Ethan chuckled. "We haven't toured for five years."

"Yeah, but our albums are still shit-hot. Come on, let's do it. Even if they have to shoe-horn me onto that drum stool I'm willing to give it a go."

"But we still have to convince Seth." Rob's expression was glum. "He can't hit the high notes for love nor money."

"We'll take the songs he'll struggle with down four semitones." Ethan ran his fingers along an air guitar. "No sweat. He won't even notice. He can't read a note of music. Baz'll be fine with it as well, as long as he doesn't get hammered. He can play any song in any key if he's sober enough. What d'you reckon, Rob?"

"Okay with me. All I'm worried about is being able to take a piss."

"That's settled, then." Mick downed a second pint then held up his right hand. "*Kickback's* back and kicking. High five."

"Kicking the bucket, more like." Rob slapped his hand against Mick's. "And this had better be the last tour. No way will I do any more."

"Absolutely." Mick nodded. "It's the beginning of the end. We've got three months to get in shape."

"Looks like I'd better start on the Finasteride then." Rob sighed. "I really don't fancy the beads yet, *or* going on stage in a nappy."

"What beads? Is it Mardi Gras?"

"Never mind."

***

Rob opened the packet of medication and skimmed through an enclosed information leaflet. Sexual function or performance could change, and pregnancy was to be avoided at all costs. Finasteride could reduce the size of a benign enlarged prostate, but it might also cause prostate cancer in the long term.

He felt he was pretty safe as regards an unwanted pregnancy, but the fact that he was considering taking a tablet that might 'change' his sexual performance and even give him cancer as a bonus was surely a no-brainer? However, he needed to be in tip-top shape for the tour, and he could always stop taking it after the tour and have the injection of beads instead.

Rob threw caution to the wind and the information leaflet into a nearby bin. He popped a tablet into his mouth and hoped the old chap would not let him down at a crucial moment.

CHAPTER FOUR

Barry Aldous opened one eye, saw the clock showing twenty minutes past two, and winced at the shrill noise blasting in his right ear. He picked up the phone's receiver, and for a blessed moment silence reigned supreme.

"What?"

"Baz, it's Ethan."

"It's two o'clock in the morning!"

"No, in the afternoon. You been on a bender again?"

"Shit." Baz sat up, clutched his aching forehead and looked to his left at Lorraine's pristine side of the bed. "What day is it? The fifteenth?"

"Seventeenth. You've missed a day somewhere."

"Fuck. Where's Raine?"

"No idea, mate. Listen… can you help me out? I need your axe. We're touring in September."

"Raine's booked me into rehab. She's had enough. She said if it didn't work out this time, then she's going. Got to check in on the nineteenth, so I had a few drinks beforehand, like."

"Just a few? Get your arse on tour with us. More money than you can shake a stick at. Mineral water for the rider though… keep Raine happy, eh?"

"I'll be in rehab until the end of August."

"Download our songs. It'll give you something to do instead of group therapy. We can have a week of rehearsals when you get out."

23

"I can't stand group therapy. I don't want to sit there with a bunch of winos talking about why I drink. I don't *know* why I drink. I just like doing it."

"Then like doing something else. Listen Baz, you know she'll walk. Do the rehab. See you when you get out. Download the lot, 'cos we don't know which songs we'll do yet. We're dropping the keys four semitones for the old songs. We've already done that on the new album anyway, 'cos Seth's voice is shot."

The line went dead. Baz replaced the receiver and flopped back on the pillows. He had the mother of all headaches. Just as sleep threatened to once more ease his pain, a finger poked at his chest. He opened one eye to the force that was Lorraine Hozier.

"Well?"

"Sorry, Raine. It won't happen again. I'm on the wagon now."

"Yeah, right." Raine sucked her teeth. "For your information, I moved out while you were circling the airport. I came back to give you my key, so here it is. Stick it up your arse, or wherever it'll do the most good."

"H-.hang on!" Baz struggled to an upright position. "I'm going to rehab next week... give me another chance!"

"Up yours."

With a toss of her red waist-length hair, the love of his life marched towards the open bedroom door and then slammed it shut behind her.

***

"I'm Baz, and I'm an alcoholic."

"Hello, Baz." Eleven falsely jovial voices replied as one. "Welcome."

Baz gave a nervous laugh after finding himself uncharacteristically at a loss for words.

"So...er... is this Alcoholics Unanimous? If I can't decide whether or not to go on a bender, somebody here will talk me into it?"

"No, we won't do that." A serious-looking middle aged man next to him wearing khaki shorts and tee shirt shook his head. "Just phone any one of us if you're struggling, and we'll come to your home to support you. We're all equal here at *Calmedron*, we've all got the same problem, and we all help each other."

"I've tried before to stop drinking, but it's hard." Baz looked at the group of strangers before him. "But this time I've *got* to do it. My wife's just left me."

"I've been there." An older man with bags under his eyes nodded. "Say... have I seen you before somewhere?"

"He's famous." A pale faced young woman with bleached blonde hair raised her right thumb. "I'm Julie, by the way, and he's Ronnie. You play guitar with Orange Transporter, don't you, Baz?"

"I *did*." Baz shrugged. "They sacked me after I went on one bender too many."

"I *thought* I heard an electric guitar." A slim man of medium height and with salt and pepper hair and flushed features grinned at Baz. "I'm Steve Isaacs. Your room's next to mine."

"Sorry if I've been keeping you awake." Baz reached forward and held out his right hand. "I've got to learn over fifty *Kickback* songs before the end of August."

"*Kickback's* my favourite group." Steve shook Baz's hand. "Can I come in and listen? I can sing 'em for you as well. I've got all their albums. My mum always said I had a good voice."

"Not until I've learned them." Baz chuckled. "Thanks for the offer though, Steve."

"It's good to have a distraction." Serious Khaki nodded. "I'm Lewis. I play online Chess. I've been sober for three months now."

Baz glanced towards a woman in her fifties who had raised her right hand.

"I'm not a drinker, but my husband Tim is. My name's Louisa. Tim doesn't want to attend meetings, so I'm here in his place. I don't stay here though, obviously."

"I'm sure I'll get to know all of you in time." Baz looked from one to the other, and to his horror felt tears burning the back of his eyes. "I only arrived last night. I'm seeing the doctor after this and the psychiatrist after that. I'm desperate for a drink already."

"You'll get some Revia to help with the cravings, and the doc will organise some blood tests to check your liver and other stuff. I'll sit with you, all night if you like." Lewis put an arm around Baz's shoulders. "But I'm not getting in your bed. You're not my type."

"I'm no shirt-lifter either." Baz, sweating now, took some deep breaths. "This is the third stint in rehab for me. This time it's *got* to work."

"And it *will*, because you want it to." A forty-something woman with fair hair tied back in a ponytail sat forward in her seat. "I'm Veronica. You'd better not call me that, though."

"Okay, Veronica." Baz managed a weak laugh. "I'll try not to."

A strong wave of nausea overcame him. Baz made his excuses and ran to his room to throw up in privacy. Hanging on to the bathroom wall, he realised that getting dry for good this time was surely going to take much resolve and strength. He hoped to all the gods in the universe that he had the staying power to see it through.

***

Trying to sleep while suffering tremors, sweats, and another industrial headache was proving impossible. Baz sat up, swung his legs over the side of the bed, and glanced at the digital clock; 02:38. Flashes of Raine on the beach, in his arms, or staring at him from the side of a stage played havoc with his addled brain. He needed a drink, and right now he would kill for one.

He walked forward to where he had left his guitar propped up against a chair. He would bust his pooper and learn the set list to distract from thoughts about beer and brandy chasers. His fingers struck the first chord of '*You Get on my Tits*':

"You've left me in bits

You get on my tits

How could I know

You were planning to go?"

He gave a *tut* of annoyance and started again in the new key. Steve's voice echoed through the thin wall.

"I love your face

Your leather and lace

But you give me the shits

You get on my tits."

Baz laughed through his pain; yeah, the guy had a passable voice. Steve's mother had been correct. When he heard a light tap on his door, Baz opened it to find a grinning Steve clad only in pyjama bottoms.

"Ready for an all-night jamming session? I can't sleep again, so it'll help me think about something other than whisky."

"Mine's beer, brandy, or anything I can get my hands on. You can help me out with verse three if you like. I've forgotten the words." Baz nodded. "Come on in."

***

Birdsong heralded the dawn, along with completion of the first song on the set list. Baz set his guitar back on its stand and yawned.

"So…how long have you been in this place?"

"About two weeks, I think. I've lost count." Steve shrugged. "I'm feeling a bit better now I've stopped drinking. After the divorce I hit the bottle hard. I didn't even know what day it was when I first arrived. My brother Bernie found me and brought me here. He saved my life, I think. I'm on the dole now. I lost my job as well."

"Well, Steve, my old lady decided enough was enough while I was off on a bender, but I didn't believe her. When I woke up, she threw the door keys at me and left."

"Welcome to my world, mate." Steve nodded in sympathy. "What will we do without them, eh?"

CHAPTER FIVE

"Roll down and touch your toes to begin with. Let's see what you can do."

With some difficulty Mick Stephenson bent forwards and then downwards with arms outstretched. To his horror he found he could only bend his body about halfway, as his back refused to move any further.

"Sorry, darlin' ". Mick raised himself up again, "I can't get down there anymore."

"That's why your GP sent you to *me*. If I can get you moving again with physio then you might not need the facet joint injections, but Pilates is not a quick fix and you'll need to keep doing the exercises and not give up." Anthea Price gave a thin smile. "*And* ...I'm *not* your darling, okay?"

"Okay, darlin'."

Mick had never met such a tight-arsed, unpleasant woman in his whole life. She looked a million dollars, but as far as he was concerned she had all the personality of a dead slug.

"Let's get you down on the mat."

"*That's* what I've been waiting to hear you say."

There was no hint of a crack in her features. Mick flopped down onto the exercise mat and tried to forget that his back was on fire.

"Lie down flat, then hold one knee and pull it up to touch your chin."

"You must be joking. My gut's in the way."

"Just try, and *do* decrease the gut in your spare time... as quick as you like actually."

Pilates had obviously been invented by a sadist. Mick grabbed his right leg and wondered how anybody could raise a knee up to touch their chin unless they were a contortionist. The woman was demented, he was certain of it, unless *she* was a sadist as well.

"It ain't happening, darlin'. I can't get it up there."

"I have a name... it's *Anthea*. Hold that stretch for a count of thirty, then do the same with the other leg. It'll help your back. Breathe in as you change legs, then exhale as you pull up."

He was certain nothing in the world could rectify the damage he'd done to himself after 45 years of bashing drums, especially lying flat out on a Pilates mat and trying to do the impossible with his 60 year old body. Mick took hold of his left knee and raised it as far as he could. The air escaped from his lungs as he mentally counted to thirty.

"That's right. Now turn over on your front so that you're on all fours."

"Isn't that what *I'm* supposed to say to you?" Mick chuckled, then turned over as instructed.

"Exhale, drop your head down and arch your back up for a count of thirty, then exhale again as you lift your head and let your back drop down for another count of thirty. Repeat a few times."

This one was easier, but he was buggered if he knew whether to breathe in, breathe out, or not breathe at all. What difference did it make anyway? He decided not to bother about all that malarkey, and just concentrate on the exercises.

"Now sit on your ball."

"I don't think so." Mick guffawed. "You've got to be joking, eh?"

"The *gym* ball that I asked you to bring."

"Oh yeah." Mick got to his feet and retrieved the ball, which had rolled into a corner. "I got a bit worried there for a minute."

"You know, it would help a lot if you didn't turn everything I say into some kind of sexual double-entendre." Anthea sighed. "It gets a bit wearing after a while."

"Just trying to lighten the atmosphere a bit." Mick shrugged. "If you like, darlin', I won't say anything at all."

"*Now* you're talking sense. Please sit on the *gym* ball and move gently around in circles. Don't forget to roll the opposite way too. These have been a few warm-up exercises you can do. In a minute we'll start on the real thing, just in case you thought you'd finished."

All his attempts to make her laugh had failed, and now she was hacked off. To be fair, he knew she was a class above the usual women who fell for his charms, but jeez... she was wound up tighter than a crab's arse, and that was watertight. Mick rolled around on the ball and tried not to stare at Anthea's legs in their tight shorts. Had she ever heard of *Kickback*? Hmm... doubtful. Thirty years ago women threw their underwear at him. Now they threw their knickers at some long streak of piss who had not even started to shave. Nobody under the age of forty knew or cared about Mick Stephenson's thirty minute drum solos. He needed to get back on stage and show them what they'd been missing, but first… first he had to sort out his back. If Pilates was the way to do this, then he'd better stop pratting about and get on with it.

CHAPTER SIX

"Seth's number's flashing. I've made you a drink." Sonia Stephenson put a glass of iced lemon juice beside the phone.

"No beer?" Mick snorted and gave the lemon juice an evil eye.

"You're on a diet, remember?"

From the floor of his in-house gym, Mick signalled to Sonia to put the ringing phone onto speaker mode.

"Yo!"

"Hey Mick, how's it going?"

"Is that *you*, Seth?" Mick gasped and reached up for the lemon juice. "I'm lying here trying to put my head up my arse."

"Sounds interesting. I suppose it's only kinky the first time you do it?"

"It ain't kinky, believe me. It doesn't sound like you, mate." Mick sat up on his exercise mat and wiped his forehead. "Your voice sounds a bit different."

"I've had some bloody awful treatment. I reckon I'll be ready to start rehearsals soon. How about you?"

"Cool. I've been doing this Pilates shite for about six weeks now. I had to have a steroid injection a fortnight ago, which helped more. Anthea the Physio is hell personified."

"Whoop-de-doo-dah. *Kickback's* coming back! I've had some filler, Rob's still taking his tablets, and Baz gets out of rehab next week. Ethan says he's okay to play rhythm. I guess it's my place or Ethan's for rehearsals then?"

"Yeah, but don't forget yours is in the arse end of nowhere surrounded by sheep. Still, your sex life should be improving then?"

"No end, Mick, no end. Are we just doing the old songs and the ones from the new album?"

"I don't think Ethan's written any more, otherwise he would have sent them to us."

"Okay. I don't care either way. I'll leave it with you to contact the others and find out where we're all going to meet up."

After Seth had ended the call, Mick gulped down the rest of the lemon juice, got to his feet, and tapped Rob's number on speed dial. Maddie's strident voice assailed his eardrums.

"He's in the loo, Mick."

"Still?" Mick chuckled. "When's he due out?"

"We all have to *go*. He's not as bad as he was, thank God. Hold on, he's coming now… it's Mick for you, Rob."

"What d'you want, you bastard?" Rob's voice sounded as low as his bass guitar. "You still owe me ten quid."

"How's your dick?"

"Bigger than yours."

"You wish. Listen… looks like it's rehearsal time. Seth's or Ethan's place? Where d'you fancy staying for a month or so?"

"I hear Seth's got two swimming pools. I'll vote for Seth."

"Oh yeah, I'd forgotten about that. I'll tell Ethan and Baz to meet at Seth's. It's great the band's getting back together."

"Yeah. You still owe me ten quid though."

"I'm good for it, so my accountant says. I'll see you in Wales then."

"Righto, Boyo."

***

"He's in his studio, Mick." Cindy's voice was a flat monotone. "I'm not allowed in there, and he doesn't answer his mobile if he's writing."

"You okay, Cind?" Mick ventured to ask, hardly expecting a reply.

"Not really. We're splitting up. I've got to move out when I've found another place."

"Sorry to hear that. Just knock on the door, tell him it's *me*, and ask him to pick up the landline."

"Okay."

Mick waited on the line for a full five minutes before he recognised Ethan's voice, which sounded a tad weary.

"What?"

"How's it going, mate? A couple of months of rehearsals. Seth's place …probably starting next week."

"Thank fuck for that." Ethan sounded more upbeat. "I can't wait to get away. I've written some new verses, but haven't touched the guitar for a few weeks… been trying to stop the pain in my elbow. I'll be okay to play rhythm though."

"Seth will send us a text and let us know the date and time."

"Bring it on."

***

"*Calmedron Rehab.* Can I help you?"

The woman sounded as though she had just finished a long course of elocution lessons.

"I'd like to speak to Barry Aldous, please. Sorry to trouble you, but his mobile's switched off."

"Who's calling?"

"Mick Stephenson."

"Hold the line. I think he may be in group therapy, but I'll check for you."

Mick drummed his fingers until Baz boomed down the line.

"It wasn't me, and I can prove it!"

Mick laughed out loud.

"Put that beer down. Rehearsals start next week at Seth's place. He'll send a text."

"I'm as sober as your mother." Baz cleared his throat. "Can I bring my mate Steve? I've met him in here. He can sing backing vocals and hasn't got any job commitments. We've pissed off the entire place every night re-learning the songs, 'cos neither of us have been able to sleep much. We know 'em backwards, forwards and sideways. Well…we did before of course, but I haven't played them all for a while."

"Check with Seth first before you bring him. My mother's ninety four now, but in her younger days she could have drunk you under the table. See you next week."

CHAPTER SEVEN

The September sun still had a sting to it. Baz felt a great weight had lifted from his shoulders as he meandered through the Shropshire hills and then crossed the border into North Wales. On the back seat of his car sat his trusty Ibanez guitar in its travel case, a battered flight bag of casual clothes, and his old Mesa Boogie amp. Raine was 300 miles away in London presumably looking for a house, which of course he would feel obliged to provide. He felt well, and free of the frequent headaches that had plagued him in the past.

"Nice scenery." Steve looked out the window and nodded in appreciation. "Thanks for letting me tag along."

"Wasn't up to me." Baz shrugged. "Seth agreed, but it's just for rehearsals, right? And there's no money in it, but you'll get bed and board."

"Who wouldn't take this opportunity? But don't worry, I'd die of fright if I had to get on that stage at Wembley."

"The chap who usually helps us out with vocals, Eddie, is on tour with another band. He'll be along in a couple of weeks."

"Great. Is that Eddie Greenway?"

"Yeah."

"Wow." Steve relaxed back into the passenger seat. "This'll be like a holiday for me. I don't usually go on holiday now, 'cos these days I don't have anyone to go with. Hey, I can't wait to meet the others. As you know, I've been a fan of the band for years."

Baz followed the satnav as it took them along a winding country lane fringed with overhanging trees. On both sides of the road sheep grazed on lush green grass.

"I think Seth's place is around here somewhere. It's called *'Cartrefol'*. I visited it a couple of times when Ian from Orange Transporter lived here. Ah, we've arrived at the postcode. The house is white with a roof like a castle, as I remember. Keep your eyes peeled."

"I see it." Steve pointed to his left. "Over there. I reckon if you follow this road then you'll come to it. Looks like it cost a fortune. It's pretty quiet round here... what will we do for entertainment?"

"Make our own. You can go off and sightsee if you want, but us... well, the band anyway... they'll be recognised and have people's phones shoved in their faces all the time."

"Ah, yeah, I forgot about that." Steve shrugged. "I saw a sign back there that said Langollen is twenty two miles away. It's a nice town... me and my ex went there once. Perhaps I'll go back and take some snaps of Horseshoe Falls and re-live old times."

Baz pootled along slowly until he saw the familiar *'Cartrefol'* inscribed on the front of a high brick wall surrounding the property. He announced their arrival over the intercom, whereby a pair of electric gates opened. He turned the car into a long gravel driveway, and came to a stop in front of two impressive portals either side of the front door. On stepping out of the driver's seat, loud music could be heard coming from the back of the property.

"Sounds like we're the last to arrive."

"Will they want me there?" Steve climbed out of the passenger seat slowly. "Will I be in the way?"

"No, you'll be fine. We'll be grateful for some backing vocals until Eddie gets here."

Baz took his phone out of his pocket and dialled Seth's number.

"Hey, you wanker, it's Baz. I've brought Steve with me. Are you going to let us in?"

"No. Gwyneth's on her way instead."

Baz grinned when the door opened to reveal a small but capable-looking lady in her sixties.

"Come in, Baz, I remember you from the old days. They're all out the back by the swimming pool." Gwyneth turned to Steve. "I'm Gwyneth, by the way. I'm the housekeeper."

"He's Steve." Baz pointed to his left. "He's star struck. I didn't realise Seth had kept you on, Gwyneth."

"Oh yes, he did, thankfully. There's food and drink out by the pool. Baz, do you remember the way?"

"I might have been out of my box last time. You'd better refresh my memory, Gwyneth."

Baz, with Steve in tow, passed through a lobby decorated with checkered black and white tiles. A large fireplace took up one wall, over which hung a stag's head complete with antlers and a disconcertingly baleful gaze. Gwyneth looked over her shoulder at Steve.

"Don't you mind Arthur up there …he's harmless."

"Glad to hear it." Steve's head swiveled in all directions. "How many rooms has this place got?"

"Thirty, well…thirty one if you count the changing room down by the pool. And I have to clean them all." Gwyneth hurried along a corridor flanked on either side by closed doors, and headed towards a back lobby. "Here you are. Just go out and down the steps and you'll see them."

"I'm nervous." Steve took a deep breath.

"Boyo, they're as tame as kittens." Gwyneth's face creased into a laugh. "Off you go, the pair of you."

"Hello Wales!" Baz held both arms up, then bounded down the steps in a few strides. "Say hello to Steve, all of you. He's crapping himself!"

"Hi Steve." Rob and Maddie spoke as one, and sat up almost instantaneously from their sunbeds. "Nice to meet you."

"So you're our backing vocalist then." Seth ceased rubbing suntan lotion on Naomi's legs and looked at Steve with interest. "Well, there's nothing much going on today. Just make yourself at home. There's beer in the little fridge under the table. Ethan's got some sausages and burgers on the barbeque. I let him get on with it."

"Hi Steve." Ethan held up a sausage. "Want one?"

"Yeah, ta, but no beer. I've just come out of rehab."

"And me." Baz yawned. "We're on the wagon. Seth…why do you live in the arse end of nowhere?"

"So no-one can find us. Anyway… *you* told me about it in the first place."

"Where's Mick?" Baz looked around the pool area. "Is he here yet?"

"He still owes me ten quid." Rob settled back on the sunbed.

"Will you shut up about that ten quid!" Maddie gave her husband a playful slap. "I'm sick of hearing you say it."

"Mick's sleeping it off upstairs." Seth moved the sun cream over to Naomi's other leg. "He got here last night. I think he was a little worse for wear then as well. He'll surface sooner or later."

"Yeah, he was, and I had to drive him here." Sonia finished swimming a length of the pool and climbed out. "Hi Steve, I'm Mick's wife, Sonia. He threw up three times on the way."

"Nice." Steve grinned at Sonia. "I've had my share of doing that. No more."

"Well, good for you." Sonia, dressed in a black bikini, extended a dripping hand towards Steve. "Mick needs to listen to you. He might learn something."

"Oh, I'm no expert." Steve shook the proffered wet hand and tried not to stare at Sonia's breasts, still pert for somebody obviously in her late forties. "It was my brother who told me to give it a rest, and my liver come to that."

"Glad you listened to them."

***

"I'm the barbeque king, and all the grub's ready." Ethan waved a pair of tongs in the air. "Come and get it while it's hot."

Baz ensured he was the first arrival at the barbeque. Steve reluctantly took his gaze away from Sonia to where Ethan had cooked a variety of foods to perfection. He picked up a plate and took his place behind Sonia in the queue. Her nearness and lack of clothing caused him to have to count an imaginary row of burgers on a never ending griddle.

"How was rehab?" Ethan plonked two sausages, a kebab and a burger on Steve's plate. "Never been there myself."

"I'm okay, but I still can't sleep."

"Steve, you want to ask Eddie about his dodgy anaesthetist pal, Dave Riley, when he gets here." Sonia held out her plate towards Ethan. "Dave's the man when it comes down to getting off to sleep."

"Christ, I don't want to end up in rehab again." Steve shook his head and added some salad to his plate. "I'm done with all that... not that I was a user or anything. Booze was my downfall, but..."

"Dave the dodgy anaesthetist sells Propofol to augment his income. If Eddie has trouble sleeping after a gig, Dave or Eddie's bird Sandra gives him a liquid cosh, and Bob's your uncle and Fanny's your aunt, Eddie's out for the count all night." Sonia ladled some pasta onto her plate. "He loves the stuff."

"I can't afford to pay any dodgy anaesthetist." Steve shook his head. "It all sounds a bit iffy to me."

"It's rock and roll." Ethan laughed. "Eddie's bird used to be a nurse, so she knows how to give injections, and how much Propofol it takes to keep Eddie breathing all night. There's no after-effects, and Eddie's up with the lark the next morning. Sandra also went out with Dave for about a year. She met him at work and I think he might still got a thing for her. It's all a bit incestuous."

"Did she get struck off?" Steve took a bite of a kebab. "This is delicious, by the way."

"Cheers. No...Sandra gave up nursing to be with Eddie. He's a session musician as he can play the Hammond organ as well as sing, although we don't use the Hammond in the band. He travels all over the world and earns enough dough for both of them."

"Shame I can't play a note." Steve chewed thoughtfully. "Mum told me never to give up the violin lessons. I should have listened. Too late now."

"Move along you bastards. I'm starving." Rob shouted from the back of the queue. "What's a guy got to do to get something to eat around here?"

***

Mick was obviously feeling better. Steve, wide awake as usual, thought of Sonia without her bikini and tried to block his ears to the sounds of sex emanating from the room next door. He glanced at the digital clock on his bedside table; 02:45 and all was not well. In the good old days he'd down a few whiskeys to solve the insomnia, but now all he could do was turn his face to the wall and pray for sleep.

CHAPTER EIGHT

Steve woke at 08:50 after what he assumed had been about one hour's sleep all night. Silence pervaded the house. He padded over to the bedroom window and looked down at the back lawn, where early sunshine shone a welcome invite onto the mill-pond features of the swimming pool. He crossed over to his case, donned a pair of shorts, and with a fluffy towelling robe from the en-suite bathroom under his arm, made his way down the stairs. Gwyneth rattled teacups in the kitchen as Steve trod quietly towards the back lobby, where he found the door to the garden already open and a continental breakfast buffet laid out on a long glass table which stretched almost the width of the patio.

Birds trilled a happy morning chorus. He threw his towel onto a sun lounger and walked over to the pool. Standing at the edge of the deep end, he raised his arms to the sun before executing a perfect dive which made hardly a splash. It was only after swimming a couple of lengths that he noticed a figure had appeared on one of the sun loungers. He rubbed water out of his eyes and hauled himself out of the pool.

"Morning!" Sonia, clad only in the briefest of pink bikinis and an open beach robe, stretched out like a contented cat. "Sleep well?"

"Not really." Steve grabbed his towel and wiped his face. "Lots of noise coming from the room next to mine."

"Oh? Which room is yours?"

"The one opposite the green bathroom"

A flush crossed her features. Sonia smiled, showing perfect white teeth.

"Sorry. We get carried away sometimes."

Steve turned back to the pool and dived in, aware of Sonia's eyes on his body.

***

One by one sleep-befuddled people arrived on the patio and helped themselves to coffee and croissants before finding a sun lounger. Gwyneth strode to and fro, adding fried bacon, mushrooms and tomatoes to the buffet. Steve, now wearing his towelling robe and wide awake after swimming twenty lengths, heaped a plate full of food, picked up some cutlery, and went back to his place beside Sonia.

"Be sure not to drip on me, darling." Sonia took a sip of coffee. "I don't like men who drip."

Irritated at an inability to keep his eyes off her, Steve turned his back on Sonia and acknowledged Ethan as he flopped onto the sunbed on the other side of him.

"Alright, mate?"

"Yeah." Ethan bit into a croissant. "Can't wait to get started on rehearsals. Apparently there's a studio to die for in the basement."

"What time? Will it be today?"

"Who knows?" Ethan shrugged. "It'll happen when it happens. Seth will call us all to arms sooner or later. We've all been pretty laid-back in the past when it comes to rehearsals, but the songs get done in the end."

"Who the fuck are *you*?"

Steve was aware of a dark shadow which had fallen across his plate. He looked up to see a fifty something, overweight man of about 6ft 2 inches who towered over him.

"I'm Baz's mate, Steve. I'm here to do backing vocals."

"I *told* you who he was." Sonia let out a *tut* of annoyance. "Steve, this is my husband Mick."

"That's *my* sunbed." Mick gestured with a backward flick of his head. "*I* sit next to Sonia."

Steve bit his lip and stood up. Mick settled his large frame onto the sunbed with some difficulty as Rob and Maddie sauntered by, each with a plate of fried bacon and tomatoes.

"Don't be so rude, Mick." Maddie smiled apologetically at Steve. "Steve's here to do you all a favour until Eddie gets here."

"No problem... I'll find another sunbed. There's plenty more."

Unwilling to make a scene, Steve walked quickly to the other side of the pool and looked across at Sonia, surprised to receive a wink. He flashed her a grin and sat down, aware of Mick's gaze. To his relief he was soon joined by Baz, who gave him a wave of acknowledgement whilst chewing a bacon roll.

"How's it going?"

"I've managed to piss Mick off already." Steve chuckled as he speared a sausage. "Something tells me we're not going to be bosom buddies."

"Take no notice of him. He's probably got a hangover." Baz yawned. "He'll be okay when his headache goes. He'll bash the drums to a pulp later on, and then he'll feel a bit better."

"Ethan said rehearsals happen when they happen. Is that right?"

"Yeah, sort of." Baz nodded. "There's no set time. This is Seth's place now, so he'll call the shots. In the meantime have another swim, take a nap, or just do what you want. Keep your phone close and I'll call you when you're needed."

Disappointed at the ubiquitous *laissez-faire* attitude, Steve finished his breakfast then made his way past Ethan, Mick and Sonia towards the patio doors and the quiet safety of his first-floor bedroom. He would take a shower, grab a tee-shirt, some jeans and trainers, and have a walk around the neighbourhood.

CHAPTER NINE

Sonia Stephenson waited until Mick, sated with Gwyneth's fried breakfast, dozed on his sunbed. She piled their used crockery onto a tray, made her way to the kitchen, and deposited the tray on top of the dishwasher.

"There you go, Gwyneth. Shall I collect some more plates for you?"

"No, no, don't you worry about that. My daughter Cerys will be here to help quite soon."

Sonia smiled at Gwyneth on her way out of the kitchen. She checked the back lobby and passageway were both empty, then ran to the foot of the stairs before taking them two at a time to the first floor landing. She took off her beach robe and rapped lightly on Steve's door, which opened far enough to show Steve wearing nothing but a large bath towel around his middle.

"Hi." Sonia grinned and threw back her shoulder-length blonde hair. "Just wanted to apologise for my husband's childish behaviour."

"No problem."

"Did I catch you in the shower?" Sonia's gaze travelled downwards. "Sorry about that."

"No, I've just got out."

Steve had either failed to spot her overtures, or she had not tried hard enough. Sonia licked her lips.

"Can I come in?"

"What for?"

"So we can discuss the weather." Sonia sighed in exasperation. "Look, I've seen you staring at me, and hey, I like *you* too. Why the fuck do you *think* I want to come in?"

"Lady, I don't know what your game is, but I've no intention of becoming a punch bag for your husband's enjoyment."

"Oh, don't bother about *him*." Sonia stepped in closer. "You'll find out it's all very *live-and-let-live* around here."

"Yeah, well... if I let you alone then I'll still get to live."

"Don't be such a party pooper, darling. Let me come in and we can have some fun."

Sonia tried hard to keep a modicum of desperation out of her voice; she had never been turned down in all her 48 years. Slowly and with great deliberation, she unhooked the front clasp of her bikini top and allowed her full breasts their freedom.

"Have I got to spell it out?"

"*I* will... N. O." Steve shook his head. "I came here to sing, not shag other men's wives."

To her horror, the door slammed in her face.

***

She would not be put off. Men had always flocked to her like the proverbial moths around a flame. Was she losing her touch? Had she become too old to attract the opposite sex? She was certain she'd read the signs correctly; Steve fancied her, she was sure of it. After his last affair, she needed to show Mick that men still found her attractive. What her husband needed was a taste of his own medicine.

Footsteps on the stairs. Sonia fastened her bikini top and donned her beach robe just as Naomi came into view.

"Hi Sonia, Maddie and I are going into town to do some shopping. You can come along too if you like. I think Seth wants to organise a practise this afternoon."

"Thanks, but I'll have a swim and then sunbathe." Sonia shot Naomi her best smile. "I'm also in the middle of a good book."

She had always preferred the company of men. Shopping with Maddie and Naomi would be like watching grass grow. They would talk about their husbands, what new clothes they were going to buy, and how tedious their lives were. Sonia brushed past Naomi and made her way to the pool, where Mick was now wide awake.

"Where did you get to?"

"Just went to the loo." Sonia sat down beside Mick. "When you've got to go, you've got to go."

"Seth mentioned a practise later on. Will you be going shopping with the girls?"

"No thanks." Sonia shook her head. "If I'm allowed, I'll come and sit in with you lot instead."

"We'll only be pissing about to start with. There won't be much to hear."

"That's okay. It'll be fun to watch you all play again. Will your back be okay?"

"It had better be, hadn't it?" Mick shrugged. "It's got to last out the whole tour."

CHAPTER TEN

Steve, dressed in clean jeans and tee-shirt, put his ear to the door of his bedroom and listened; nothing could be heard. Carefully he opened the door and checked the landing both ways before making his way down the stairs. His mobile phone rang as he came within a few feet of the front door.

"Hi Baz."

"Where are you?"

"I'm just about to go out sightseeing." Steve opened the front door and stepped out. "Why?"

"You're wasting your time…there's nothing to see but sheep and cows. We drove here, remember? Listen, there's a practise this afternoon. Go down to the basement around three o'clock."

"Oh, that's great. I wondered when the first one would be."

"Could be a late night once we get going."

"No probs. Thanks, Baz. See you later."

Steve closed the door quietly behind him. From the back of the house came the sounds of music and voices. The gravel driveway now seemed much longer than when he and Baz had driven along it just a couple of days before.

He turned left out of the driveway and walked for a while along a deserted country road, enjoying his own company. Woodland stretched into the distance on the right hand side, and to his left a herd of cows munched contentedly on lush grass in a field ringed with electrified fencing.

Steve stepped onto a verge and looked over his shoulder as the bucolic peace was shattered by an approaching car, complete with honking horn. The passenger window opened.

"What you doing out here?" Maddie's mouth broke into a grin. "Naomi and I are going into town for lunch and shopping. Want a lift? It's twenty miles to Llangollen."

"I'm just out for a walk." Steve glanced at his phone and then at the empty back seat. "It's only a few hours now until the practise... I'd better not, but thanks anyway."

"Suit yourself. See you later, Steve."

Maddie pressed a button to close the window, and Naomi drove away. Steve, aware that Sonia must still be in the house, decided to continue walking until his stomach told him it was lunchtime.

***

"Wow, this is some set up you've got here!" Steve gave Seth an appreciative nod. "As good as any professional studio I'm sure."

"Cheers." Seth allowed a grin to spread over his features. "Ian King from Orange Transporter used to live here... that's his brother Billy at the mixing desk. He's a wizard with all that shit, and he'll play our songs back to us so we can hear what we sound like *now*. Baz told me about the place when he knew Ian wanted to sell and that I was looking for somewhere out of the way with a studio."

"What song's first?"

"Well ...if you turn around and take a seat on that sofa in the far corner, then we'll let you know when you're wanted."

Steve nodded and followed the direction of Seth's finger to where Sonia sat cross-legged like a latter-day Yoko Ono. Her icy glare caused a feeling in his stomach akin to that of a vertical drop on a roller coaster ride.

"Er... can I just sit nearer the lads and watch? Promise I won't make a nuisance of myself."

"Drag a chair up to the microphone next to mine then. You'll be able to use that one when we've gone over the guitar parts. Rob needs to refresh his memory a bit first, and Ethan and Baz need to get in sync."

With a feeling of relief, Rob positioned a chair that faced Seth's microphone and Mick's drum kit behind, but was sideways on to Sonia's dagger-like stare. Boredom crept in after he had listened, stock-still, for more than an hour to Rob's bass runs, but his ennui lifted in an instant as Seth finally turned towards him.

"Steve, let's see what you're made of then. We'll start with '*Pay the Price.* D'you know that one?"

"Yeah."

"Put your headphones on. Just sing a third above me for the chorus to start with."

Heart hammering in time to Mick's pounding intro, Steve stood up and donned a pair of headphones which hung over the microphone stand. From his peripheral vision he was aware that Sonia had taken a seat right next to Mick. He turned his back to the pair of them and focused on Billy the Wizard as he flicked a multitude of switches and levers. When Sonia sashayed into the mixing booth, Steve swallowed hard.

"You missed your cue." Seth poked a finger into his own chest. "Watch *me,* not Billy."

"Sorry, mate. It won't happen again."

Steve turned ninety degrees to face Seth, aware that Sonia had exited the mixing booth and had now positioned herself once again in his line of vision. He stared at Seth as though his life depended on it, and managed to complete one verse of the chorus albeit with an unusual tremor to his voice.

"No good." Seth shook his head. "I thought Baz said you could sing?"

"I *can*. It's *her*." Steve pointed towards Sonia. "She keeps walking around. It's putting me off."

Steve felt the prod of a finger in his back. He spun around to face the full force of Mick's ire.

"You having a go at my wife?"

"No, but I can't concentrate when she keeps moving about all the time."

"Sonia, can you please pick *one* seat and stay there?" Seth let out a sigh of exasperation. "Then perhaps we might get some work done."

"It's okay, I know when I'm not wanted." Sonia shot Steve one last poisonous glare. "I'm going for a swim."

The door to the studio slammed shut. Mick thumped his way back to the drums, and Steve closed his eyes briefly in relief. Seth gave Billy a thumbs up.

"Let's take it from the top again. Steve, stop pratting about and *sing*!"

Free of the pernicious influence of Sonia, Steve opened his mouth and gave *Pay the Price* his best shot, pleased at the resulting applause from Baz, Ethan, Rob, and also Billy in the mixing booth. Behind him, he was aware that Mick had steadfastly remained silent.

CHAPTER ELEVEN

Outside an owl hooted its presence in *Cartrefol*'s grounds. Seth stood alone at the mixing desk, munched on a plate of sandwiches, and listened once more to the day's practise. Sure, Steve could sing, once he'd found his voice, but their new backing singer had caused an undercurrent of tension not usually present when the band were together. Mick, normally fun-loving and easy-going, had taken umbrage and there had been an uneasy truce all afternoon between Mick and Steve.

The main door to the studio opened. Naomi made her way to the mixing desk, stood behind Seth and wrapped her arms around his waist.

"Coming to bed, babe?"

Seth turned around to face Naomi and gave her a kiss.

"Yeah, okay. I've just been listening to the stuff we've played today. What do you think of the new guy, Steve?

"He's just here until Eddie arrives, isn't he?" Naomi looked up at Seth. "Why d'you ask?"

"Something's going on. He's pissed Mick off already, and Sonia's been acting strangely. I told her to stop walking around the studio while we were practising, and she stormed off."

"She didn't want to come shopping with Maddie and me today either. Perhaps she and Mick have had a row? It *has* been known to happen, especially when he's been drinking."

"I'll have to ask him." Seth shrugged. "I can't have this bad feeling every day. Eddie's not here for another couple of weeks, and to be honest, it'll throw a damper over things if it goes on too long. Steve's a good singer though, and after today I'm thinking of asking him to sing with us permanently, but I'll have to get the others' opinions first. I'll call a meeting. Tomorrow will be a good day, as it's Sunday and we'll mainly chill until the evening. I think Mick might say *no* though, unless I can find out what the problem is."

"*You* know Sonia." Naomi chuckled and buried her head in Seth's chest. "She might have made a play for Steve. Perhaps Mick found them in bed?"

"No, surely not? He's only been here a day or so!" Seth kissed the top of Naomi's head. "She doesn't seem his type."

"Seth, if she's offered it to him on a plate, and *you* know what happened back in the day as well as *I* do, what bloke's going to say no?"

"It was only a one-off thing. I was hammered and she knew it."

"Obviously not *too* hammered …eh?"

"Let's not go into that now. If she's up to her old tricks and tried it on with Steve, and then Mick found out, well yeah, there's going to be trouble."

Seth turned off the mixer desk, and then with Naomi's help switched off all the studio lights and locked the main door. Hand in hand with Naomi whilst walking upstairs to bed, he decided to by-pass Mick, have a talk in private with Steve the following day, and get any issues out into the open.

***

The one face he wanted to see at the breakfast table was not there. Seth checked the time on his phone; 10:45. He

56

backtracked to the kitchen where Gwyneth wiped down counter tops with a cloth.

"Has Steve been down this morning?"

"Been and gone ages ago." Gwyneth nodded. "Carys and I had not been asked to take any refreshments to the studio, and so I told him this morning was definitely free. He said he'd get a taxi to Llangollen for a bit of sightseeing and be back early afternoon."

"Oh, okay. Thanks Gwyneth. I think we'll have a practise this evening though. Some sandwiches and cake will be great, if you could just leave them in the fridge before you go home. Lunch about three?"

"For sure. Mr Price, the farmer up the road, sold me a twenty five pound turkey, which I put in the oven about an hour ago."

"Sounds delicious." Seth raised his right thumb. "We'll clear the breakfast stuff while you're at church. Don't worry about that... off you go and I'll see you later."

By 11:15 everyone had finished eating. Seth tapped the side of his glass with a spoon.

"I just want to call a quick meeting before you all slope off, but first... it's Sunday and Gwyneth and Carys have gone to church. We clear our own shit up on Sunday mornings, so let's get cracking and then we can get on with the meeting."

"Us girls will do it." Naomi stood up. "It's no trouble. Get on with what you've got to say, and we'll work around you."

Seth ignored a *tut* from Sonia, who picked up her own plate, headed towards the kitchen, and did not return. He passed his dirty crockery to Naomi, who gave him a wink.

"Lads, I thought it would be a good time now to discuss how the practise went yesterday."

"No probs." Ethan shrugged. "Went okay as far as I could tell."

"Yeah, I agree." Rob nodded. "We'll be fine for the tour. It felt just like old times."

"Not sure about Steve." Mick gave a soft belch. "Why don't we get rid of him and just wait until Eddie gets here?"

"Actually, I wanted to talk about Steve. After that shaky start I thought he was fine. He knew all the songs, and he's got a good voice." Seth glanced at Mick's impassive features. "What do you say that we take him on permanently as a backing singer? Eddie often has other commitments, and Baz let me know that Steve's on the dole. We also won't need to pay Steve as much as Eddie."

"Sure." Ethan gave a thumbs up. "Makes sense to me. What about you, Rob?"

"If you like. I've got no problems with it."

"Eddie's better." Mick shook his head. "Eddie won't like getting pushed out. Steve's an alcoholic. Who knows if he'll be sober all the time, and how will he act if he has to walk out on a stage?"

"Are *you* sober all the time?" Rob grinned. "Steve hasn't touched a drop to my knowledge while he's been here."

"I don't like the prick." Mick chewed on a fingernail. "I say no."

"Three against one. Let's give him a chance. He can be on trial until the tour starts, and I'll tell Eddie we've got somebody else." Seth drank the rest of the juice in his glass. "The meeting's over for now. Let's have another practise this evening around half past six. Enjoy the rest of the day."

He handed Maddie his empty glass. Mick strode to the dining room door, threw it open, and slammed it shut behind him.

CHAPTER TWELVE

Steve could once again hear music and laughter coming from the direction of the pool area. A tantalising aroma of roast turkey filled the hallway. He ran upstairs to his room and closed the door, then opened a packet of sandwiches he had bought in Llangollen. He heard a knock on his door as he bit into the first one.

"Who is it?"

"Seth."

Holding the rest of the sandwich, Steve jumped up, swallowed a mouthful of cheese and tomato, and opened the door.

"Hi Seth."

"You don't have to buy lunch." Seth pointed to the sandwich. "Gwyneth's got roast turkey and all the trimmings about half past three. Have you had a nice morning?"

"I went to Llangollen. I wanted to see the Horseshoe Falls."

"Oh. Haven't seen it myself. I just wanted a quick word, if that's alright. Can I come in?"

"Sure." Steve held the door open wider and then closed it behind them. "Anything wrong?"

"Just wondered if anything had happened between you and Mick."

"Not Mick as such... er... it's Sonia that's the problem. She came on to me and I turned her down."

"Oh Christ!" Seth laughed out loud. "You should have said something. Naomi was right. Was that why she kept walking round the studio?"

"Yeah." Steve nodded. "So she could face *me* all the time and put me off."

"Well, that's no problem. I'll tell her to keep out when we're practising. I'll tell *all* the girls to find something else to do, so that Sonia doesn't think she's been singled out."

"She must have said something to Mick about me. I'm getting negative vibes."

"He's probably seen her looking at you. It'll blow over. Mick played away last year, and Sonia's a bit vindictive."

"Yeah, she's attractive, but I'm not about to go around shagging everyone's wife. That's not *me*."

"And we don't want another *Fleetwood Mac* drama, do we?" Seth grinned. "Anyway, another reason I came here is to ask whether, after a suitable trial of course, you'd like to sing backing vocals permanently with the band and go on tour with us in the autumn."

"You're kidding me, right?" Steve opened his mouth like a fish.

"Straight up."

"Does the Pope wear a dress? It's a chance I've dreamed of!" Steve grinned at Seth. "I won't let you down. The drinking days are behind me now. You have my word."

"That's settled then. You'll be on trial here until the tour. If everything's okay you'll get a percentage of the ticket sales, bed and board on the tour bus, and here of course, and our manager will draw up a contract for you."

"I can't believe it!"

"*Believe* it." Seth laughed. "It'll happen."

"But what about the other guy... Eddie? He won't like it that I've taken his job."

"Leave Eddie to me. He doesn't have a contract yet for this tour." Seth turned towards the door. "See you at lunch."

***

Steve took a deep breath and opened the dining room door, aware that everyone had stopped in mid-chat to regard him with interest. Rob raised one hand in greeting.

"Welcome to our new band member!"

"Thanks, Rob." Steve could not stop a wide grin. "I'm dead chuffed."

"You're on trial." Mick waggled one finger. "Fuck up just once, and you're out. Eddie'll have something to say about this."

"I don't intend to fuck up, Mick. You'll find that out. Eddie will have to jog on, won't he? It wasn't *my* decision to sack him."

"But you didn't say *no*, did you?"

"Well, neither did *you* when you were asked to play the drums."

"I look forward to touring with you." Ethan, one arm outstretched, reached across the table. "Congratulations."

Steve shook Ethan's hand, ignored the arrows of hatred shooting from Sonia's eyes, and sat down next to Rob.

"Do I get to choose a rider on the tour?"

"Of course." Rob nodded. "We all do."

"Then just mineral water for me, and sandwiches. I'm never touching another drop of alcohol."

"That's what they all say." Mick sniffed. "When you're high after a gig and can't get to sleep, then you'll need a shot or twelve of Jack Daniels. Don't come crying to me after the third night with no sleep and telling me I was right after all."

"I won't."

"Give the new guy a break, Mick!" Ethan helped himself to more salad. "Christ, you're a miserable bastard aren't you?"

"Ethan, don't start on Mick." Sonia leaned into Mick and kissed his cheek. "He's telling it how it is. Steve should listen."

"I'm listening, but if you've never been at rock bottom, staring at the dregs of yet another bottle of whisky and wondering how the hell you're going to survive another day, then you won't understand why I only want mineral water as a rider. This quiche is very good, by the way."

"It's Gwyneth's specialty." Naomi passed the plate of quiche towards Steve. "Want some more?"

"Only if there's any left over."

"There'll be none when I'm around." Mick snatched another piece of quiche from the plate. "Who gets the job of imparting the good news to Eddie?"

"*I'll* do it." Seth held one hand up. "Eddie's not being sacked as such, as he hasn't got a contract for this tour. It's just that it's more convenient for us to employ Steve."

"Hope he takes the news okay." Mick smiled enigmatically at Seth. "As you well know, he's not exactly a shrinking violet."

"Leave Eddie to *me*." Seth downed half a glass of lager in one go. "He's probably got another tour lined up anyway with one band or another."

***

Steve lay wide awake in bed, his heart still hammering with excitement. Never in all his born days had he ever expected to be given the chance to go on tour with the band he had followed since way back when. He reached over and grabbed his phone from the bedside table. His brother would never believe it.

"Hey Bernie!" Steve sat up, cross-legged. "I know it's late, but I've just *got* to tell you something."

"What?" Bernard Isaacs yawned. "Can't it wait 'til the morning?"

"No it can't. Guess what? I'm going on tour with *Kickback*!"

"What d'you mean, going on tour?"

"Singing. I'm their backing singer now."

"Straight up? Wow! How the hell did you manage that?"

"It's all down to you, big bro. You got me into rehab, and I met Baz there, who sometimes plays guitar with them."

"It's the chance of a lifetime, mate. I'll know where to come now if I need a loan."

"Not just yet though." Steve laughed. "I won't get paid until after the tour."

"Where are you? Still in rehab?"

"No, at Seth Hurley's house in Wales. It's a dream come true. I still can't believe it."

"Believe it. Well done. Glad that things are looking up for you. Can I have a backstage pass?"

"I'll see what I can do. Laters, as they say."

"Yeah. Laters. I'm going back to sleep."

CHAPTER THIRTEEN

Eddie Greenway screeched the van to a halt outside the sign 'Cartrefol', backed up a bit, then wrenched the steering wheel to the left and shouted through the intercom. Gravel flew in all directions as the van skidded to a stop outside the morning room's long sash window. Eddie threw open the driver's door and looked over his shoulder at the forty-something redhead in the passenger seat.

"Stay there, Sandra. I don't want you getting involved."

He pushed himself out of the van at speed, not bothering to close the door. When Gwyneth let him inside the house he strode with purpose as he followed her to where music and laughter emanated from the back of the house.

"What's going on, you fuckers?" Eddie spat on the floor. "You can't fire me just like *that*!"

"We haven't fired you, Eddie, you *know* that." Seth jumped up from his sunbed and quickly made his way towards where Eddie stood fuming. "We haven't given you a contract for this tour, because we've found somebody who can join the band full time."

Eddie made a fist, pulled back his right arm, and threw a punch in the direction of Seth's cheek. Seth, nose streaming with blood, took a step back.

"Fucking bastards, the lot of you!" Eddie, wild-eyed, scanned the pool party. "Who's taken my job?

"*I* have." Steve climbed off his sunbed, glad the pool was between himself and Eddie. "It's not personal. It's just that I was in the right place at the right time."

"Not personal?" Eddie ran along the side of the pool towards Steve. "How's it not personal when some nothing-from-nowhere takes *my* job and *my* percentage of the ticket sales?"

"I'm with *you*, Eddie!" Mick shouted from his corner of the patio. "Straight up!"

"No-one's *nobody*." Steve stood squarely in front of Eddie. "Everyone's *somebody*, even a bastard like *me*."

Eddie, panting now, hurled himself towards Steve, who stepped lightly to one side and then dived, fully clothed in shorts and tee-shirt, into the deep end of the pool and swam its entire length underwater. Seth, Ethan, Baz and Rob, working as one, hauled Steve out at the other end. Eddie ran to where the five men stood together.

"You're welcome to stay the night, Eddie." Seth held up one hand in reconciliation. "But I don't want any trouble. Steve stays. It's also a question of economics, as I told you on the phone. You wanted a higher percentage, and that's just not feasible. By the way, where's Sandra?"

"In the van." Eddie glowered at Steve. "What's it to *you?*"

"Naomi, run round and get Sandra, and tell Gwyneth there'll be another two for dinner." Seth walked forwards, wiped the blood from his nose with a sleeve, and put one arm around Eddie's shoulders. "Come on, mate, as Steve said, we're not doing this for the fun of it. It's nothing personal."

"You're all bastards." Eddie shrugged out of Seth's clutches. "I never thought you'd do this to me. I've got huge outgoings, and three kids at private school and two at university to keep. I haven't got another tour arranged until next year."

Sorry mate. Manny says we have to watch *our* costs as well."

***

Gwyneth placed a large container of salad foodstuff in the middle of the dining table.

"Chicken legs are on their way, as are the baked potatoes."

"Thanks Gwyneth." Ethan's gaze followed Gwyneth's retreating back until she had left the room. "Jeez, it's like a pox doctor's waiting room in here."

"It's Steve that's upset the apple cart." Sonia glanced around the table, then focused on Steve. "We were okay until *he* arrived."

"We were okay until *Eddie* arrived, you mean?" Rob speared a piece of cucumber with a fork. "It seems we're likely to spend more time arguing now instead of practising."

"Look. If I'm causing the friction here, then perhaps I should go." Steve faced each person in turn around the dining table. "What do you think?"

"Suits me." Eddie sat back in his chair.

"*And* me." Mick grinned at Sonia, who nodded.

"No-one's going anywhere tonight. We'll sit at this table and eat like the civilized and reasonable adults we are, and then we'll have a practise after dinner, around eight o'clock." Seth stood up. "I'm going to help Gwyneth bring in the rest of the food."

"Sandra, us girls can go to the cinema room later on while the boys have a practise. We'll put on a chick flick." Naomi's eyes followed Seth as he walked towards the kitchen. "Want to sit with us?"

"Thanks for the offer, but no." Sandra shook her head. "I'll just walk about and explore a bit before I have to sit in the van again tomorrow for another six hours."

"I'll show you around, Sandra." Sonia shot Sandra a smile. "I'm not much for chick flicks."

Eddie drummed his fingers on the arms of his chair until all the food had been brought in from the kitchen, noticing how Steve had seated himself furthest away at the other end of the table.

"So what am *I* supposed to do tonight when there's a practise then?"

"Eddie, you can either sit in with us and listen, have a swim, watch TV, or go to bed. It's entirely up to you." Seth helped himself to a chicken leg. "Dig in, people, while it's all hot."

"Yeah, I'll sit in, I think. I'd like to listen to this new shit-hot singer, and see what *he's* got that *I* haven't. But don't worry... we'll be out of your hair in the morning."

"I think I'll pass on the practise tonight." Steve cut through a baked potato and added some grated cheese on top. "There'll be plenty of other sessions. I'll go for a swim instead."

"You can all suit yourselves." Seth added some salad to his plate. "Or you can all fuck off. I don't give a shit."
***

Angry that his chance to stare at Steve and put him under pressure had been thwarted, Eddie still could not resist the urge to join his erstwhile band mates in the studio. At eight o'clock he and Sandra walked hand-in-hand past the swimming pool, where Steve steadily swam length after length.

"Sonia told me to wait for her here, so I'll grab a sunbed, wait for Sonia, and then we'll walk our dinners off around the grounds." Sandra let go of Eddie's fingers and found herself a sunbed. "You go... I expect Seth's already arrived to open up the studio."

Eddie glared one last time at Steve, who so far had ignored their presence, and then made his way to where Seth, Ethan, Baz and Rob had already congregated at the studio door.

"We're going to try out a couple of Ethan's new songs, so you wouldn't have known them anyway." Seth flicked on the studio lights. "It's just a jamming session, Eddie, not much happening tonight."

"I'll sit in for a while anyway, if that's okay with you."

"Whatever." Seth sighed. "Just do what you want."

***

Increasing fatigue had taken over from his earlier endorphin-fuelled swim. Steve lay wide awake in bed and stared at the digital clock's display on the wall opposite: 00:46. Outside on the landing Eddie and Sandra's voices made no concessions to the late hour.

Steve, at his wits' end, could not bear one more night without any sleep. He climbed out of bed, quickly put on a pair of shorts and a tee shirt, and then opened the bedroom door.

"Eddie." Steve hissed through clenched teeth. "Can I ask a favour?"

"Fuck off." Eddie opened his bedroom door and ushered Sandra inside. "You've already had my job. What else do you want?"

Steve padded across to the end of the landing where Eddie still stood outside his room.

"Can I have some of that stuff you get from your doctor? Ethan told me about it. I can't pay you, but I do have a Rolex watch that my brother gave me when I agreed to go to rehab. You can have that, or sell it if you like."

"I've already got one."

"So sell it then. Come on... I'm desperate. *Please*."

"Why should I do anything to help *you*?"

"I don't know."

"The only time I'd give you any stuff is if you'd agree to piss off and let the rest of us get back to normal."

"Yeah, okay." Steve nodded. "I'll do it."

"We've got enough Propofol for him, and I'll ring Dave and ask him to bring some more." Sandra whispered from just inside the bedroom door. "You'll get to sing with the band again, Eddie."

"Go back to your room then. Lie down on the bed." Eddie waggled one finger in his direction "Just this once though, and I expect you to leave tomorrow."

"Yeah, okay." Steve came to the conclusion he would let Seth and the band decide his fate, but the lure of unconsciousness was too good to ignore. "I'll go as soon as I wake up."

He didn't like needles at the best of times, and his heartbeat increased at the sight of Sandra coming in through the bedroom door holding a syringe full of what looked like milk.

"This won't take a minute." Sandra tapped the back of his right hand with her fingers. "Keep squeezing and making a fist. You've got nice big veins. Shut your eyes, and I guarantee you won't feel a thing. Have a good sleep and a safe journey home tomorrow."

Steve closed his eyes and awaited the arms of Morpheus. He did not have to wait very long.

CHAPTER FOURTEEN

The late summer sunshine felt warm on the back of her neck as Gwyneth made her way across *Cartrefol's* gravel driveway the next morning. She unlocked the front door, then reached inside to turn off the burglar alarm. The house was silent, as was usual at such an early hour of the day.

She bustled about in the kitchen, preparing the continental breakfast the band always enjoyed. Sunlight streamed in through the window, and she decided to once again arrange breakfast savouries outside on the long patio table. She unlocked the back door, then picked up a tray of clean glasses and stepped outside.

Birds trilled the arrival of a new day. Gwyneth took in a deep breath of summer air and headed towards the table. Sparkles glinted off the pool, and Gwyneth screwed up her eyes against the brightness. She took a longer second look at an unfamiliar shape floating on the top of the water, and then dropped the tray and screamed in fright.

The glasses shattered into a myriad of shards on contact with the concrete patio. Gwyneth, shouting for help as though her life depended on it, ran back through the door and upstairs towards the bedrooms, where doors flew open and sleepy people emerged yawning onto the galleried landing.

"What's happened?" Seth, clad in just pajama bottoms, scratched his head.

"It's Mister Steve!" Gwyneth struggled to catch her breath. "He's floating face down in the pool!"

"What!" Seth forced his feet into slippers. "Are you sure, Gwyneth?"

"Go and look, boyo." Gwyneth panted. "See for yourself!"

"I'll call an ambulance!" Ethan tapped the keyboard of his mobile phone. Mick, Rob and Baz, all clad in dressing gowns, hurried down the stairs towards the patio, while Maddie, Sonia and Naomi rushed to Gwyneth's side.

"It's too late… too late." Gwyneth crumpled into a sobbing heap on the floor. "He's *dead*. I know he's dead."

***

Attracted by the sound of three police cars arriving, along with a private ambulance, interested rubberneckers had already crowded around *Cartrefol's* gates. Gwyneth, comforted by Naomi, Maddie and Sonia, sat on a sunbed and sipped sweet tea. Seth stood by the pool in stunned silence as the doctor put away his stethoscope and undertakers laid Steve's body out on a stretcher underneath a velvet coverlet of the deepest purple, on which a long yellow crucifix had been etched.

"I just can't believe it." Seth shook his head. "What the hell has happened here?"

"Beats me." Mick shrugged. "Eddie said he'd seen him swimming up and down last night. As you know, we don't go this way from the studio up to the bedrooms, so I just assumed he'd gone to bed while we were at the practise."

"Did anybody see *anything*?" Seth fought hard to hold back tears.

"Not a thing. It was dark and a bit after midnight when we left the studio." Rob shook his head. "As Mick said, we didn't need to go back this way. The police will want to speak to us in a minute, now their chap's finished examining Steve."

"Yeah, he was swimming up and down when I sat here waiting for Sonia." Sandra sat next to Eddie, his arm around her shoulders. "I didn't see him after that."

"It looks bad for *me* because I wanted him out of the way." Eddie took a deep breath then exhaled slowly. "But hey, I wouldn't have done the bloke in. Yeah I felt like punching the guy, but I've got five kids and all their mothers depending on me *not* to end up in prison."

"Don't mention those bloody mothers ...they're the bane of my life." Sandra looked up at Eddie. "Why couldn't you keep it in your pocket?"

"Sorry, babe. It's what being on the road does. I'm going to have to explain all this to the cops now... they're coming over."

An older cop and a youngish-looking policewoman, dark hair carefully crafted into a bun, walked around the side of the pool towards them.

"I'm WPC Lynda Marriott, and my colleague is Detective Inspector Simon Williams. Shall we go into the house? There's quite a crowd gathering outside. We don't want anyone from the press creeping about and listening."

"Of course." Seth nodded and turned towards the house. "Follow me. We can sit in the dining room."

"I'll lay some breakfast stuff out. Gwyneth's not up to it at the moment." Naomi rushed past Seth. "Girls... do you want to help me?"

***

"Let's start from last evening." D.I Williams opened up a notebook. "The Coroner's officer informs us that Mister Isaacs died between the hours of nine o'clock last night and two o'clock this morning. When was the last time anyone saw him?"

"My wife Sonia and I saw him around eight o'clock." Mick's hands shook slightly around a cup of coffee. "I was on my way to the studio, and Sonia was waiting about by the pool for Sandra... they had agreed to go for a walk."

"I'll need to speak to those two ladies, and the housekeeper who found him." WPC Marriott looked around the table. "Where are they?"

"In the kitchen." Seth pointed one forefinger over his shoulder. "None of us have had any breakfast yet, and our housekeeper is a bit distressed. The girls are preparing some food and looking after Gwyneth."

The policewoman stood up and made her way towards the kitchen. D.I Williams leaned back in his chair and regarded the rest of the group.

"There was an empty bottle of whisky on a table by the pool, and Mister Isaacs was found clothed in a tee shirt and shorts, not swimming trunks. The forensic guys will check the bottle for fingerprints, and will take blood tests and samples from the body. Was Mister Isaacs in the habit of swimming in his clothes whilst under the influence of alcohol?"

"He was on the wagon." Baz shook his head. "He'd just come out of rehab. I know, because I'd been in rehab with him. I'm Baz... er...Barry Aldous. No way would Steve have touched another drop of whisky. He'd just got a job with the band, and was looking forward to changing his life around."

"Well, we'll check his stomach contents and his blood alcohol level. We'll soon discover whether he'd fallen off, so to speak." D.I Williams jotted a few words in his notebook. "You say he'd been in rehab? Baz ... had Mr Isaacs been prescribed any medication to help him cope with the withdrawal symptoms?"

"Same as me, probably, although we didn't speak about it. One tablet of Revia for a twelve week period. I'm still taking mine, and I guess so was Steve. I expect the worst thing he could have done would be to mix whisky with the Revia and then go swimming, although I'm sure he didn't as he still had his shorts and tee shirt on. It was dark outside and so perhaps he fell in?"

"I see." D.I Williams scribbled down more notes. "Thanks for the information. Did Mister Isaacs have any enemies? Was there anybody he'd fallen out of favour with?"

"I'm going to own up before you hear it from someone else." Eddie slightly raised his right hand. "He'd been given my job. I didn't like it and I raised a few objections, but hey, I'm no killer. He was alive when I last saw him."

"And that was...?" D.I Williams regarded Eddie with interest.

"Around eight o'clock. I'd said goodbye to my wife, who was going for a walk with Sonia, and I went to the studio where the band were due to have a practise. Steve was swimming lengths at the time."

"I saw him at dinner, around an hour or so earlier." Rob stood up to take a tray from Maddie containing several cups of coffee. "He was a bit quiet and said he wanted to miss the practise."

"I'd come on a bit strong and said I wanted to listen to him sing. I'd have been stressed out just the same as Steve if I'd been in the same situation… who wouldn't?" Eddie took a cup from the tray. "I was an arsehole yesterday. I regret it now."

"Can anybody else add anything?" D.I Williams looked from one band member to the other, and then at Ethan. "How about you… er…"

"Ethan Taylor. I'm lead guitarist with the band. Like Rob, I only saw Steve at dinner last night. He tended to keep himself to himself. I think he felt a bit like an outsider, as he'd not long joined us."

"Well, you've all been very helpful. Stay around here, because we'll be back when we have the results of the forensic tests. My team and I will carry on doing our thing here for a while longer, and we'll take DNA samples from all of you for the process of elimination. We'll search Mister Isaacs' room, and we'll contact his family." D.I Williams stood up. "But just for now I'll leave you all to your breakfast."

***

Muted conversations hummed around the breakfast table. When the last of the food had been eaten, Eddie wiped his mouth with a serviette and looked at Seth.

"I guess Sandra and me will be off now."

"You can't." Seth shook his head. "The police told us all to stay here. You might as well take part in the next practise if you like."

"So now I'm second best?"

"No, you're the arsehole that you just said you were." Seth sipped the last of his coffee. "*We* need a backing singer. *You're* a backing singer. Work it out."

"I'll think about it." Eddie stood up. "I'll let you know."

"Do that, but don't take too long."

***

"Have you got a moment, ladies?"

WPC Marriott entered the kitchen. The housekeeper sat stoic and silent on one of the breakfast bar stools and every now and then brushed away a few more tears. She saw four other women busying themselves scraping plates, loading the dishwasher, and wiping down surfaces.

"Sandra Greenway?"

"That's me." Sandra stood up straighter. "How can I help?"

"Where was Steve Isaacs when you last saw him?"

"Swimming lengths." Sandra put down the plate she carried. "I was supposed to meet Sonia by the pool after dinner, but she didn't show. I sat there at the pool for about twenty minutes, and then went for a walk on my own after that."

"Not with your husband?"

"No, he went to the studio."

"Did Steve talk to you at all?"

"No."

Try as she might, WPC Marriott could not stop waves of irritation washing over her every time Sonia Stephenson flicked back her mane of obviously bleached blonde hair.

"When did you last see Mister Isaacs, Mrs Stephenson?"

"At dinner. Something I ate gave me a headache, probably the cheese I put on the baked potato. I don't usually eat cheese. I took an Aspirin and had an early night. Next thing I knew Gwyneth was shouting on the landing outside."

"And you, Mrs Tayor?" WPC Marriott regarded Maddie. "Where were *you*?"

"In the cinema room with Naomi. We watched a film." Maddie looked at Naomi for confirmation.

"Yes, that's right." Naomi nodded. "The boys were still practising when the film ended, so I had a shower and went to bed."

"So did I." Maddie agreed. "Rob came up about half past midnight."

WPC Marriott turned her attention to where Gwyneth still sat in silence.

"Gwyneth, do you live on the premises?"

"No." Gwyneth shook her head. "I live on my own in the village, a short walk away, but my daughter is nearby with her family. I know the code for the gate ... it's the same as it was when Mister Ian King lived here, and Mister Hurley changed the locks but lets me have a key. I used to work for Mister King too, and he trusted me and so gave me a good reference."

"What time did you leave last night and enter the house this morning?"

"I put all the crockery in the dishwasher after dinner, and then went home about eight thirty. I only stay late if Mister and Mrs Hurley have guests... I usually go around three o'clock. I came in about half past seven this morning, I was just going to unload the plates and stuff and put the breakfast things on the table outside when I saw poor Mister Steve floating in the pool." Gwyneth dabbed her eyes again. "Such a tragedy."

"Indeed. Thank you Gwyneth, and thank you ladies." WPC Marriott put her notebook away. "We have enough to go on at the moment, but once the results are in I'm sure we will be back again soon to question you all further."

   ***

"What's your impression?" D.I Williams closed the driver's door and started the engine.

"Strange about the clothes he was wearing." WPC Marriott fastened her seatbelt. "Why no trunks?"

"Yeah, I thought that too. He must have fallen in."

"Or was pushed?"

"Apart from the Eddie guy, who seems genuine enough, no-one seems to have had any ruck with him." D.I Williams put the car in first gear and pulled away. "And who drank all that whisky?"

"I'll be interested to find out the results of the tests and the autopsy."

"Me too. If there's no alcohol in his blood, then someone else has either drunk the whisky or left that empty bottle there on purpose."

CHAPTER FIFTEEN

David Riley had never had anything good happen to him in Wales. Now, because Sandra was stuck, he'd had to give up his weekend golf and drive hundreds of miles to some godforsaken Welsh village just to offload some more *milk of amnesia*. Granted, the remuneration was worth it, but his face, not to mention the Maserati, would stick out like a sore thumb in a place where everyone knew everybody else.

The Maserati was almost as wide as the country lane. Dave made a mental note of each passing place as he sped by, but as luck would have it he saw no other car for the final three miles up to *Cartrefol's* closed gates.

Two people, one with a camera, mooched around outside. Dave opened the electric window of the Maserati and pressed the intercom button.

"Hi, it's Dave."

He took a quick glance at the two men. One of them raised the camera towards him and clicked the shutter.

"Excuse me, have you anything to say about the death?"

"What death? Stop taking pictures! Who the hell are *you*?"

The gates creaked open. Dave closed the car window and drove down the driveway at speed. In the rear view mirror he could see the two men running behind in a vain effort to catch up. He grabbed a gym bag and jumped out of the car when he saw Seth at the door.

"Who are those two?" Seth looked beyond Dave to where the man with a camera clicked as he ran. "The police are here again, luckily. I'll get them to arrest those pair of wankers for trespassing."

Dave followed Seth into the house and closed the door. Outside he could hear footsteps on the gravel.

"Press maybe? They mentioned a death. Who's dead?"

"A backing singer."

"Not Eddie?"

"No, not Eddie." Seth sighed. "*Steve.* You didn't know him. He drowned in the pool."

"Christ!" Dave hitched the bag higher on his shoulder. "I've got some more stuff for Sandra... you know. She said Eddie's run out."

"Keep it to yourself." Seth whispered. "That's all we need... the police getting hold of that bloody bag. They're in the dining room, just about to give us the results of Steve's autopsy and forensic tests."

"Shit. If I'd known they'd be here I wouldn't have come."

"*We* didn't know until a short while ago. No worries. I'll say you're our tour manager."

***

Dave, bag clutched tight to his shoulder, followed behind Seth to where two police officers sat at the dining table and faced the rest of the band. Motioning Dave to take a seat, Seth took a chair next to Dave.

"Sorry for the interruption. This is Richard Trent, our tour manager."

"Hi." Dave slid the gym bag under his chair. "I'm just staying until tomorrow."

"D.I Williams, and my colleague WPC Marriott." Simon Williams looked Dave up and down. "So ...what do *you* do then?"

"Oh, er... this and that." Dave shifted about in his seat. "Book venues for the band to play, mainly."

"So where have you booked so far?"

"He actually managed to get us into Wembley, which we're thrilled about." Seth coughed and gave Dave a pat on the back. "Cheers, mate."

"*Anyway...*" D.I Williams checked his notebook. "Getting back to Mister Isaacs, tests reveal that no alcohol was found in his bloodstream. The Coroner states the autopsy showed he didn't die from drowning. He was already dead when he hit the water, as his lungs were more or less clear. His death is therefore suspicious and will need to be investigated further as a possible homicide. My team are on their way. We have a warrant to search the premises, and you'll all be interviewed individually. Please stay here at the house, and that includes you, Mister Trent."

"I've only just got here." Dave shrugged. "I've got nothing to do with all this. I don't even know who you're talking about."

"That's for *us* to decide." D.I Williams put the notebook in his top pocket. "You're part of the band, and you might be able to give us information that you don't think is important *now*, but you never know ... at a later date it could help us move the investigation along."

Dave kicked Seth's foot under the table and received an answering nudge.

***

"Seth, why the fuck did you say I was your tour manager?" Dave ran one hand through his thick black hair. "I'm a bloody anaesthetist! What do I know about running a tour, for fuck's sake? I need to get rid of this gear in the bag and then get back to work!"

"Spur of the moment thing, mate. How could I say you're here to send Eddie to La-La land? I'll tell them you've got nothing to do with it and to interview you first." Seth dug one finger in the side of the bag. "We can't have this stuff hanging around... the cops will find it."

"What the hell do you suggest I do with it then?" Dave hissed through clenched teeth and watched DI Williams through the patio window as he and the policewoman skirted around the swimming pool. "Sell it on eBay? And when they interview me what the hell am I going to say?"

"Say you're here to discuss ticket sales and how much we're going to make from the tour. Go and flush the stuff down the bog. Put the syringe in the medicine cabinet, rinse out the phial and stick it down your pants or something. They won't search there. If they find the syringe I'll say it's there just in case. Eddie will just have to stay awake a little while longer."

"Why don't you stick it down *your* pants?"

"It's my house, you wanker, I might even be the chief suspect. Go on upstairs... quick...second one on the right...while they're outside and before the others get here."

Dave made his way through the dining room and up the stairs to the landing. The door to the bathroom was locked.

Dave kept a keen watch on the stairs until he heard the toilet flush. Sandra emerged from the bathroom.

"Sorry Sandy, Seth's told me to flush the stuff down the toilet. Too risky."

"Eddie really needs it." Sandra sighed. "When can you bring some more?"

"Not yet. Why have you run out so soon? I gave you enough last time to last a few weeks. What have you done with it?"

"I... er... Eddie uses more now." Sandra looked with longing at the gym bag. "He can't get to sleep without it."

"He'll have to wait." Dave went into the bathroom. "Bugger off. I need to go to the loo. I may be in here a while."

"Don't get rid of it, Dave."

"I have to, sorry. It's the end of my career if the police find this. You mustn't give Eddie any more than the usual dose. If you do, it might kill him."

"I didn't." Sandra sighed. "Steve wanted some. He was desperate. He said if he got some and had a good night's sleep he'd go home the next day and leave it free for Eddie to sing."

"I did wonder if somebody else might have wanted it." Dave slipped in quickly behind the bathroom door. "Anyway, it's too late now to worry about it. Just go downstairs and carry on as normal."

CHAPTER SIXTEEN

D.I Williams did not have much of an idea what tour managers might look like, but this Richard Trent was no Peter Grant. Nor did he resemble Colonel Tom Parker either. The man in front of him was around 5 ft 9 inches, with black hair that flopped over his forehead, and thin to the point of anorexia. He also appeared decidedly nervous.

"Mister Trent. You arrived today, did you not?"

"Yes, and I need to get back to the office."

"What for?"

"I have a team to oversee." Dave bit the side of a fingernail. "It's all go at the moment, what with a tour to arrange."

"I see."

D.I Williams concentrated his stare on the man in front of him, who shifted about impatiently in his chair.

"Did you know the deceased?"

"No, Sir, as I said before, I'd never seen him or heard of him."

"Yet you're the tour manager? Surely you'd know the band members?"

"Well, yeah, the main ones, but they'd just taken him on I think, a matter of a few days ago."

"Where are you based, Mr Trent?"

"London…South London. I'm just here for a day or so to talk about the finances… ticket sales, the band's percentage and all that."

"All that?"

"Well… you know."

"No, I don't."

"Things that tour managers talk to bands about." Dave sighed and wished he did not feel a keen sense of foreboding. "Where they want to play first, for instance."

"And how much was Mister Isaacs going to get paid?"

"He'd get a percentage of the ticket sales. The tickets haven't all been sold yet. Perhaps you'd like one?"

"Not my thing, I'm afraid." D.I Williams shook his head. "So you'd never even met Steve Isaacs?"

"That's correct. Is it possible I could get back to London and catch up with my team soon?"

"You can, but we'll need a telephone number and the address you'll be at, just in case we need to contact you."

"Yeah, I'll write them down for you, and then I can go?"

"For now, yes, but stay close to the phone." D.I Williams took the piece of paper and then regarded Trent over the top of his glasses. "And don't leave the country."

As soon as Trent had made a somewhat hurried exit, D.I Williams sent a text to his office with details of Trent's address for verification. He had one of his gut feelings; something about the bloke bothered him, but he couldn't put his finger on exactly what it was.

***

The following day he'd already decided Seth Hurley would be his next interviewee, but his mobile phone rang before he could even climb into the car. D.I Williams picked up his bag with one hand and checked the number display with the other.

"Stu… what's the problem?"

"No problem, Sir… it's just about that address you gave us to check out."

"What about it?"

"Well, the house is registered to a Doctor David Riley."

"Not Richard Trent?"

"No. I'm going over there this morning to see who's about."

"If he opens the door and he's skinny, with black hair and about five feet nine, then I'll need to speak to him again. You'll have to bring him back here to the station."

"Righto, Sir. What's he done?"

"Don't know yet, but I'm going to find out."

D.I Williams ended the call, got into his car, and sped off to '*Cartrefol*'. He announced his arrival and curbed a stab of irritation on hearing Gwyneth's voice over the intercom.

"They're all still in bed, Mister Williams. It's only half past nine."

"You'll have to get Mister Hurley up. I'd like to speak to him."

"I can't go into his bedroom, Mister Williams, it's not proper."

"Knock on his door, Gwyneth, but let me in first."

Simon Williams drove up to the front door, which Gwyneth had already left ajar. He stepped into the hallway to meet a dishevelled Seth descending the stairs wearing only a dressing down, and followed by Gwyneth.

"Mister Hurley, I need to speak to you."

"Good morning." Seth yawned. "What's the problem?"

"Let's go into the front room. Do you want to get dressed first?"

"No, it doesn't matter. Gwyneth, please could you bring us some coffee?" Seth smoothed down his hair as he turned to Gwyneth. "Thanks very much."

Simon Williams took a quick glance around the grandiose room, and wondered whether he'd been in the wrong job all his life.

"I've had some news from the office. Do you still have Richard Trent here on the premises?"

"No, he went home last night." Seth tied the belt of the dressing gown a little tighter and then sat down. "Take a seat. Why do you ask about Richard?"

"The address he gave me is registered to a Doctor David Riley. Why is that, please, and what sort of doctor is Mister Riley?"

Williams was certain he'd seen a flash of something or other akin to nervousness pass briefly over the man's features.

"He lives with his husband. David owns the house I suppose, but I'm not sure what his specialty is."

"I've sent a man of mine to check it out. Perhaps our Richard and David have had a little pillow talk."

"Who knows? Actually, I think I *would* like to get dressed now."

Gwyneth, bearing a loaded tray, made her way into the living room. Williams took a cup of coffee from the tray as Seth stood up.

"I won't be long. I think I need to get some trousers on for decency."

"Okay."   D.I Williams raised his cup. "Don't be too long. I'll wait."

CHAPTER SEVENTEEN

Seth grabbed his mobile phone from the bedside and locked himself in the en-suite bathroom so as not to wake Naomi. After a quick speed-dial he was relieved to hear Dave's voice down the line.

"Hi Seth. What's up?"

"Dave, why the fuck did you give your own address to the police? They're sending someone round to you this morning."

"Shit! I'm at the hospital now and just about to go into the operating theatre and scrub up. Which address *should* I have given then? I don't have three homes like *you* do, and who the hell knows where Richard lives?"

"*I* do. Who'll be there to answer the door?"

"Kerry, my bird. I'll have to clue her up to what's going on."

"Dave, I've had to tell Williams you're gay and that you live with Dave Riley."

"Oh, cheers for that. Anyway, it's a bit hard for me to get away from him, don't you think?"

"Don't be facetious. They think you're Richard, so you'll have to tell Kerry."

"She's as thick as shit. She won't cope with the questioning."

"Just tell her what to say. I've got to go. Williams is waiting downstairs."

Seth washed his face, combed his hair, and put on a pair of jeans and a top. He replaced the phone on the bedside table, and his coffee was still warm when he returned to where Williams was found in the process of checking out the large DVD collection.

"Found any to your liking?" Seth drained his coffee cup and sat down on the sofa.

"No. Not my type. Too graphic." Williams returned to an armchair. "Just for your information, we questioned a Miss Kerry Hawes early this morning. I've just had a phone call. Kerry is quite adamant that nobody by the name of Richard Trent lives at the address your tour manager gave me. The owner is a Doctor David Riley, an anaesthetist, who is her on-off boyfriend. At the moment it's obviously *on*."

"I don't know anything about that." Seth shrugged as his heart raced. "Perhaps he's got two houses?"

"She then gave my team a photo of David Riley, who when they sent it to my phone looks remarkably like the man I spoke to only yesterday. In fact, I'd say in court that it *is* David Riley, who now for reasons known to only *him* seems to be calling himself Richard Trent. I've told my team to bring Mister Riley up here again with proof of ID for more questioning, so that we can find out what's really going on. You also need to get in touch with the real Richard Trent and bring *him* here as well, with proof of *his* ID. I can get my team to investigate Trent's whereabouts, but I'm sure you have his number in your little black book."

Seth could feel beads of perspiration spring up on his forehead. Williams' gaze was unflinching.

"Sure, but I know as much as you do." Seth drummed the fingers of one hand against the arm of the sofa. "I think there's been a mix up somewhere."

"Apparently the team has to wait to apprehend Riley because instead of selling concert tickets, he's currently in the middle of a radical neck dissection."

"Poor guy."

"Who? David Riley?"

"No." Seth shook his head and struggled to keep eye contact. "The person having his neck cut open."

"Mister Hurley, please stop pratting around and phone Richard Trent *now*, in my presence."

"My phone's upstairs."

"Use the landline."

"Yeah, I can, but Richard's number is stored on my mobile."

"I'll come upstairs with you."

"My wife is still asleep." Seth's effort to keep his voice from wobbling was fading. "My phone is in the bedroom."

"Keep the door open and come straight out again."

Seth stood up on legs that felt like jelly.

"Come with me, then."

The game was up, and outside the press were closing in like vultures. Naomi, naked as the day she was born, sat up in bed as Seth came in the room.

"I heard voices. What's going on?"

"Cover yourself up." Seth hissed. "D.I Williams is on the landing."

"Why?" Naomi leaned forward towards the door.

"Never mind." Seth picked up his phone. "Just go back to sleep. I'm sorting it."

CHAPTER EIGHTEEN

It had been a long operation, but now the patient had been wheeled to Recovery. Dave sat back in his seat and wiped sweat from his forehead as a scrub nurse entered the theatre.

"Doctor Riley, a WPC Marriott has phoned three times. She's sent someone from the Welsh Police to wait for you outside the operating theatre. I think it's urgent."

Dave resisted the urge to turn around and look through the door's glass porthole. There was no other way out of the theatre except through the main entrance, and a couple of staff members who had overheard the scrub nurse were already looking at him with more than a passing interest.

"Yeah, okay, thanks." Dave stood up with a feeling of impending doom. "I'll go and see what they want."

Sweating even more now, Dave pushed open the door and came face-to-face with the 6ft 5inch solid wall of muscle that was Constable Peter Evans.

"Doctor Riley?" PC Evans pushed an ID card in front of Dave. "I'm PC Peter Evans of the Welsh Police Department. There's been a new development in the Steve Isaacs' murder case, and we'll need to bring you back to Wales to ask you some more questions at the station."

"Sure." Dave nodded. "But it's been a long day and I need a shower and to get out of these scrubs. Something to eat would be good too. Any chance of all these before I leave here?"

"If you're quick. I'll wait for you in the changing room. And you have ID on you?"

"Yeah."

There was no escape. Dave wondered if the one phial of Propofol he had managed to stash in his lunchbox at the bottom of his locker would be unearthed when he opened the door to grab his clothes. If so, apart from a large amount of money currently residing in his Swiss bank account, he would be well and truly fucked.

***

The journey back to Wales was taking somewhat less time than previously. Dave sat in the back of the police car and closed his eyes against the glare of headlights on the A40.

"Where am I staying tonight?"

"Get some sleep in the car. We'll get to Wales early morning time. D.I Williams wants to ask you some questions."

Dave, fatigue washing over him, fell asleep almost immediately. He awoke several hours later with a crick in his neck and a full bladder as PC Evans brought the car to a halt.

"We're here. The others will be arriving soon. We'll get you some breakfast and a cup of tea or coffee."

"Cheers."

His legs felt stiff. Dave sniffed the crisp early morning air and wished he could outrun the brick shithouse walking too close to him for comfort.

"Am I under arrest?"

"Not as such." PC Evans held open the station door. "Just helping us with our enquiries at the moment."

"I don't know anything other than what I've already told you."

"That's to be seen. You can wait in the interview room for D.I Williams to arrive. In the meantime I'll show you where the bathroom is, and then you can have some breakfast."

Dave, famished, finished off two bacon rolls and a cup of coffee in record time. He nearly choked after starting on the second cup when Evans and Williams came into the room, accompanied by Seth and another man whom he did not recognise.

"We meet again." Williams nodded to Dave. "All of you take a seat and I'll begin a recorded interview. Doctor Riley, do you know the other man here who is accompanying Mister Hurley?"

"Never met him before." Dave shook his head.

"So why, when previously asked your identity, did you call yourself by his name? We have the real Richard Trent here."

"I didn't, Sir. If you recall, somebody else did. Perhaps they obviously got me mixed up with Mister Trent."

"So why didn't you correct them? Mister Trent is stocky and has red hair and a red beard and you are slim, clean-shaven, and have dark hair. I can't see how the two of you look similar in any way."

"I let it rest as I thought correcting the name might look a bit suspicious. After all, I assumed you were conducting some sort of enquiry."

"What are *you*, an anaesthetist, doing hanging about with a rock band?"

"I'm a friend. Originally one of the fans, but then I got to meet the band when I won a competition ten years ago to name their new album. We hit it off and have been friends ever since."

"PC Evans obtained permission yesterday to search your locker whilst you were having a shower. Would you like to know what he found?"

"What?" Dave swallowed a small amount of bile which had risen in his throat.

"Hidden inside your lunchbox was a phial of Propofol, which we have discovered is a strong sedative used in surgical operations. Doctor Riley... are you stealing sedatives from the hospital where you work for either your own or somebody else's use?"

"No... I was going to put it back..." Dave took a deep breath against a wave of nausea. "I... I..."

"Doctor Riley, I am arresting you with theft of NHS hospital property, and illegal use of anaesthesia or intent to supply. You have the right to remain silent, but anything you say may be used against you in a court of law. You have the right to legal representation. If you do not have a lawyer, then one will be found for you. Do you understand?"

"Yes."

"Tell me... how long does Propofol stay in the body for after an operation is over?"

"Between two and twenty four hours." Dave's voice sounded unusually croaky.

"So it's entirely possible that you *could* have supplied Propofol to Mister Isaacs. Did you *administer* Propofol to Mister Isaacs as an aid to sleep?"

"Absolutely not." Dave shook his head. "I wasn't even there when he died, was I?"

"Wasn't you?"

"No."

"If you weren't there, then who was?"

"As I said, I don't know *who* was there. All I know is that I *wasn't*. This is an outrage. I am a professional anaesthetist who just came up here to be with my friends. You have no proof Mister Isaacs died from an overdose of Propofol."

"No, because you made sure you used an anaesthetic that didn't stay in the system for too long."

"I think I need to get in touch with my lawyer." Dave stared Williams in the eyes. "I'm not going to say any more."

***

"Mister Hurley, why did you give me a false name for Doctor Riley, when he and Richard Trent look so different?"

Seth fidgeted about on his chair and avoided any eye contact.

"Not sure. Could be loads of reasons... I'd had a late night and was tired, I know that."

"And *I* know that you wanted to keep Doctor Riley's profession a secret, so you said he was your tour manager."

"You don't know that at all." Seth crossed his left leg over his right and swung it back and forth under the table. "You're just guessing."

"Mr Hurley, unless you tell me the truth, you might be going to jail with *him* as an accessory to involuntary manslaughter." D.I Williams pointed one finger at Dave. "And then you'll have to kiss goodbye to any tour you had planned. Tell me also why there's a syringe in your medicine cabinet. Was it for the administration of Propofol to either yourself or to somebody else in the band?"

"I have a needle phobia. I don't go anywhere near syringes or needles." Seth watched an ant crawl across the Formica table. "A few years ago one of Naomi's little nieces had some Calpol when she was staying with us, as she had a fever. Naomi squirted the stuff down her throat with the syringe, and so I think it's probably from that time, although we'd have washed the syringe out afterwards."

"How convenient."

"Don't know about convenient, but it's true."

***

"Mister Trent, so far you've been silent in all this."

"You haven't asked me anything." Richard Trent cleared his throat and made eye contact with Williams. "What do you want to know?"

"Are you aware of anyone in the band who has a Propofol addiction or who has trouble sleeping?"

"No." Richard shrugged. "I don't live in their pockets. I just arrange the tours and deal with the finances."

"Do you know Doctor Riley?"

"No, I've never seen him before."

"Yet he says he's a friend of the band?"

"Perhaps he is." Richard took a quick glance at Dave. "I don't know all their friends. How could I?"

"Do *you* have trouble sleeping?"

"No, not usually."

"Who does, then?"

"I don't know. You'll have to ask the band themselves."

"I'll do more than that. I'll check their medical records. Records aren't subject to amnesia or untruths... they're there in black and white. Evans... get the team on it. Take the good doctor to the station and get a copy of his bank statements for the last few years. Speak to the band, get their GPs, and let's have a look at who can't sleep at night and who might know how to inject Propofol."

"Righto, Sir. Will do. Come with me, Doctor Riley. You'll be able to phone your lawyer from the station."

CHAPTER NINETEEN

D.I Williams drove slowly past the gaggle of press outside *'Cartrefol'*.

"Anybody charged yet, Sir?"

"Have you any information for us, Detective Inspector?"

"No comment." Williams pressed the intercom. "It's Williams. Please open the gate."

Mindful of trespassing laws, none of the journalists followed behind his car. D.I Williams ignored questions shouted at him from the other side of the gate, and smiled at Gwyneth as she opened the door.

"I'm here to speak to Edward Greenway and his wife."

"He's with the others in the studio. Sandra might be with him. I'll go and find them, if you wait in the morning room."

Williams sank into an armchair. The room had become familiar to him now, and he had no inclination to look around. Within a short time voices sounded in the hallway, and the Greenways came into the room. Williams decided there and then that the pair of them appeared decidedly edgy.

"Hi." Eddie sat on the sofa and Sandra took a seat beside him. "How's it going?"

"It's going well." Williams gave the couple a smile that did not quite reach his eyes. ""So… Mister Greenway… it's taken a few days, but we've done our homework." Williams waved a sheaf of papers in Eddie's direction. "I'll get straight to the point. We've found out that your GP has supplied you for years with sleeping pills of various strengths, yet we've found none of them in the room that you and your wife have been staying in."

"I don't take them anymore." Eddie shrugged. "I don't need them."

"Why is that?"

"I sleep better now."

"Have you ever had Propofol administered to help you sleep?"

"What's that?"

"It's an anaesthetic."

"No."

"Mrs Greenway...you're an ex-registered nurse who used to inject patients as part of your job, yes?"

"I haven't practiced as a nurse for quite a few years now." Sandra glanced nervously at Eddie. "I'd be a bit rusty these days if I had to inject anybody."

"It appears Mister Isaacs' medical records show he had trouble sleeping too. Have you ever injected your husband or Mister Isaacs with Propofol?"

"No, of course not." Sandra shook her head. "How would I get hold of any in the first place?"

"Via Doctor Riley." D.I Williams scanned Sandra's face very closely for a reaction. "Is that true?"

"No, it isn't."

D.I Williams placed a pile of bank statements in Eddie's hand.

"Mr Greenway... could you explain the regular withdrawal of hundreds of pounds in cash over the last ten or so years, as shown in these statements?"

"God knows." Eddie sighed. "I'm a session musician... a singer. New microphones, P.A systems, tour expenses... could be anything."

"What about a few cheques in the past we've seen that you'd made payable to Doctor Riley?"

"No idea." Eddie shook his head. "He's a friend... could have been for holidays we went on with him and his ex."

"Where did you go?"

"Usually the Caribbean."

"As you know, Doctor Riley is still in custody until tomorrow. I *will* check that information right now."

"Whatever."

D.I Williams took advantage of a resulting silence to take his phone out of his pocket and tap in a number.

"Evans? Is that you?" Go and ask David Riley if he ever went on holiday with Edward and Sandra Greenway, and if so, where they all went. Get back to me as soon as you can."

Williams decided to let the pair of them stew until Evans returned the call, which finally came after ten agonising minutes. After a brief conversation he replaced his phone in his pocket and wrote in his notebook.

"What did he say?" Eddie sat forward on the sofa.

"Saint Lucia."

Williams desperately wanted to wipe the smirk off the couple's faces, but that could wait until another day. He needed to make it worthwhile so Riley might admit who was buying the Propofol, but right now it was time to go back to the station and charge the not-so-good doctor with theft. The hospital were willing to press charges, and so they could at least get Riley banged up on one count anyway.

***

"You can't keep me here another day without charging me."

"Yeah, yeah, Doctor Riley, all in good time." D.I Williams sat down on the only chair. "Listen... you know you could be up for involuntary manslaughter, which will be a much longer stretch than just nicking Propofol. I could also add in drug smuggling, and conspiracy to pervert the course of justice for good measure as well, if you like."

"I haven't killed *anybody*."

"Yeah, but you *supplied* the stuff. It was in your locker. Who bought it from you? Come on Doctor... I *am* going to charge you, but you could get a reduced sentence if you're willing to give us some more information. Mister Isaacs' medical records show he was a chronic insomniac, and so is your mate Eddie Greenway. Which one of them bought the Propofol?"

After four days to think about his plight, Williams knew that Riley might well have realised he'd lost everything and would end up in some godforsaken halfway house at the end of his jail sentence, stacking supermarket shelves for an income. He'd also doubtless already had quite enough of the claustrophobic prison holding cell, the thin, back-breaking mattress, and the lack of privacy to perform his usual bodily functions. Williams waited with baited breath.

"They *both* did, although I didn't get any money from the dead guy. Perhaps he paid Eddie, I don't know. Sandra rang me and asked me to bring some more because Steve had asked for some. Okay? So...how long will I get then?"

Williams felt like punching the air.

"Conrad Murray, if you remember him, got four years and was out after two. You may get less as you didn't give the Propofol injection to Mister Isaacs, you only supplied it. This brings me to the next question... who *did* inject it?"

"Sandra, Eddie's wife. She's an ex-nurse. She's done it for years."

"And will you testify in court to this?"

"Yes." Dave nodded. "As long as you keep to your part of the bargain."

"That's agreed. So why do you think Eddie hasn't died but Mister Isaacs did?"

"I expect she gave him too much. Eddie's a big bloke and Steve, well I didn't know him personally, but maybe he was shorter and slimmer and didn't weigh as much as Eddie. She's probably used to giving the same dose all the time. Eddie could have carried the body down to the pool to make it look like a drowning. Without Propofol, Eddie's going to need weeks of rehab to be able to sleep properly."

"He'll get help in one of the prison hospitals I'm sure. I'll send my guys to pick him and his wife up. Thank you for your honesty. Evans will read you out the charges. See you in court."

CHAPTER TWENTY

Sandra snuggled up to Eddie's warm body and threw one leg across his thighs.

"Dave won't say anything, will he?"

"Depends."

"On what?"

"Sandy, he won't want to go to jail. What would *you* do? He's probably been singing like a bird all day. We'll most likely end up having to do the same and blame Dave. We'll say he sneaked in overnight."

"The police can track Dave's whereabouts on the day Steve died. They'll *know* he wasn't here."

"But they can't *prove* what happened. They never found any stuff here at the house, other than what was in Dave's locker, and there's no solid evidence or DNA to suggest we had anything to do with it." Eddie yawned. "I was careful when I carried him down to the pool, and we washed our clothes straight away."

"Yeah... but..."

"If we're arrested and there's a trial, we can just say we're innocent. Isn't that what they *all* say in court? Prisons are full of innocent people. It was an accident after all, you didn't set out to kill him, and both of us didn't realise he might have needed less stuff than *I* do. God, I could really do with some of it now… I don't think I'm ever going to sleep again. Anyway, we'll give the jury something to think about, won't we?"

"If you say so, Eddie."

"Yeah, I *do* say so. Stop worrying and go to sleep."

***

Noises outside on the landing. Eddie, wide awake, turned towards the bedroom door as it opened to reveal the silhouettes of two uniformed officers. He cuddled a still-sleeping Sandra closer to him, and scrunched his eyes against the sudden glare of bright spotlights above.

"Edward and Sandra Greenway, you will both be arrested and charged with the involuntary manslaughter of Steven Keith Isaacs, and also with perverting the course of justice. You have the right to remain silent, but anything you say may be used against you in a court of law. You have the right to legal representation. If you do not have a lawyer, then one will be found for you. Do you understand?"

Sandra stirred in his arms. He could see Seth and Naomi hovering outside. Eddie faced D.I Williams and Peter Evans.

"Yes, but we haven't got any clothes on."

"W..what's going on?" Sandra heaved herself up on one elbow. "I don't know what's happening here."

"Cover up." Eddie draped the sheet over Sandra's shoulder. "You're showing too much flesh."

"Get yourselves dressed. I'll wait outside."

Eddie did not want to take his arms from around Sandra. Who knew when they would be together again? One thing he *did* know… if Dave and the rest of the band stayed schtum and the jury decided in his favour, he would check himself straight into rehab. He would do *anything* for just one night's proper sleep.

***

Eddie sat in the dock of Chester Crown Court, flanked on either side by Sandra and Dave, and studied the jurors' expressions as the clerk of the court asked the foreman to stand up. From their impassive stares he could see not a single inkling of the outcome that would determine their lives for the foreseeable future. He gave it up as a lost cause, and took a quick glance up to the public gallery, where Seth, Rob, Ethan, Mick and Baz all gave him a thumbs up. From the amount of noise outside, police were obviously having some difficulty in keeping *Kickback* fans from storming the building.

"And have you reached a unanimous verdict in the case of The Crown versus Edward Timothy Greenway?" Justice Lionel Butler-Curtis surveyed the jury."

"Yes, we have." The foreman nodded.

"Do you find the defendant guilty or not guilty of aiding and abetting the involuntary manslaughter of Stephen Keith Isaacs and perverting the course of justice?"

"Guilty, Your Honour."

Eddie took a deep breath as he felt Sandra's hand slide on top of his.

"And have you reached a verdict in the case of The Crown versus Sandra Marie Greenway?"

"Yes, we have."

"Do you find the defendant guilty or not guilty of the involuntary manslaughter of Stephen Keith Isaacs and perverting the course of justice?"

"Guilty, Your Honour."

Sandra's fingernails dug into the back of his hand. Eddie closed his eyes as a hush settled over the court.

"And lastly in the case of The Crown versus David Matthew Riley, do you find the defendant guilty or not guilty of theft of a controlled drug, Propofol, intent to supply, and perverting the course of justice?"

"Guilty, Your Honour."

Judge Lionel Butler-Curtis pounded the desk with his gavel.

"This case is dismissed. Prisoners will return a week from today for sentencing. Officers, take the prisoners down."

CHAPTER TWENTY ONE

"So now we haven't got *any* backing singer at all." Seth moved nearer to the microphone. "Testing, one, two, three."

"We'll be okay, just the five of us." Rob turned on his amp and then checked the tuning on his guitar. "Hey, what about asking one of the girls? Linda McCartney did a good job in Wings."

"Maddie's tone deaf." Rob laughed. "What a *racket*."

"Sonia can't sing a note." Mick shook his head while practising a drum roll. "She'll hate me for saying that."

"Raine can't stand the sight of me." Baz flexed his fingers. "She's buggered off."

"So has Cindy, but she's got a great voice. She sings all the time. Drives me mad sometimes." Ethan tried a run in A minor and winced. "She'd love the chance, I'm sure. She'll look good on stage too."

"So what are you waiting for? Ring and tell her the glad tidings." Seth waved his microphone in Ethan's direction. "*After* the practise though, and I take it *you* don't want the job, Naomi?"

"Bloody right I don't!"

"I'm getting nervous. It's been a long time since we played live." Rob let his fingers run up and down the bass fretboard. "We're just a bunch of old has-beens."

"Speak for yourself, but hey, all the venues are sold out." Baz laughed. "I'll be pushing my walking frame all the way to the bank."

"We're as old as we feel." Seth raised his arms above his head. "And right now I feel about twenty five. Okay, my voice is pushing sixty years old and now and again it needs a shot of steroid, but the rest of me isn't."

"It bloody well is." Naomi laughed. "Who do you think you are? Peter Pan?"

"No... I just feel *good.*"

"That's because we're productive again instead of sitting about growing old." Ethan played a power chord. "I'm a bastard if I've got nothing to do. Well... Cindy says I am, anyway. She'll be surprised to hear from me."

***

"Cind?"

"What?"

"Sorry I've been such a prat."

"You can't help it, Ethan."

"Listen... I've got a question for you."

"The answer's *no.* I've got a new boyfriend. At least there's only *two* of us in the bed every night, and I haven't got to worry about whether or not your tuning keys will end up poking my bloody eyes out."

Her words were like a punch to his chest. Ethan took a deep breath.

"It's not about *that.* Good luck to you. The question is whether you'd like to sing on stage with the band. You must know all the songs by now, and the gig at the Utilita Arena in Birmingham is only a few weeks away."

"Where's Eddie?"

"It's a long story. He's away, and won't be around for a couple of years."

"You really want *me* to sing?"

"I'm *asking* you, aren't I? You'll have to come to Wales to Seth's house and practise though."

"You'll never manage another tour. You're all too old."

"That's where you're wrong. Seth's on steroids, I've got Baz to help out, Mick does his physio exercises every day, and Rob's on meds."

"What about Jeffrey?"

"Who the fuck's Jeffrey?"

"My boyfriend. He's twenty five and hunky. He won't want me to meet up with *you* again."

Bastard!

"Who gives a shit *what* he thinks? Do you want to sing or not? There'll be money for you to buy some flash clothes, and we'll book you into hotels. You won't have to sleep on the tour bus."

"Thank Christ for that."

"Is that a *yes*, then?"

"I'll talk it over with Jeffrey and let you know."

"Jeez, Cind. We haven't got much time left. You'll need to get up here pretty quick if you want to do this."

"I can't just walk out on Jeffrey, can I?"

"Yeah, you can. Just *do* it."

"I must say… going on stage would be a dream come true for me."

"There might be some A&R men in the audience to snap you up."

"Oh, okay then. When do you want me to start?"

"*Now.* Get your arse down here to Welsh Wales."

"Give me the address. Can Jeffrey come? He can take a few weeks off work. He's a bouncer at the nightclub where I first met him."

"Oh, bloody hell, Cind. Who wants *him?"*

"*I* do."

"As soon as he kicks off or gets in the way, he's out. And… he'll have to pay his own hotel bills."

"You're all heart. See you soon."

CHAPTER TWENTY TWO

Cindy, holding Ethan's hand, followed the torchlight to where steps led up to the back of the stage.

"This is it, guys. We're on." Seth turned around to face the band. "Group hug."

"I'm nervous." Cindy wobbled on her high heels. "They won't like me."

"'Course they will." Ethan put one arm around her and the other around Seth. "You look just like Stevie Nicks."

"Who's *he*?" Cindy pouted. "You're telling me I look like a bloke?"

"She's priceless, Ethan." Rob moved the circle in closer with his arms. "We're going to *kick ass* tonight."

"I'm going to *throw up* tonight." Cindy closed her eyes and felt many breaths on her face. "I can't believe I agreed to this."

"You've left me in bits…" Seth sang out loud above the general noise.

"You get on my *tits*!" Cindy laughed and broke away from the huddle. "Yeah, Ethan, *you* get on my tits."

"But you love me really. Come on, time to go up."

Cindy could hear rhythmic clapping and chanting from the audience. She ran towards the front and peeped through the safety curtain.

"They're doing Mexican waves out there."

"Yeah." Ethan fastened the strap more tightly on his guitar. "They always do. Get back next to Mick."

Cindy ran to the back of the stage. Her earpiece felt strange and her mouth was dry. She took a quick swig of water from a bottle on the floor next to her microphone. A deafening roar exploded from the crowd at the same time as fireworks shot out from both sides of the stage and the safety curtain opened.

"A- one, a – two, a – one, two, three, four!" Mick beat time with his drumsticks, Rob flicked his fingers up and down the fretboard, and Cindy heard Ethan's opening chords to '*Gotta Get me a Woman*' followed by the sound of Baz and his wah-wah pedal making the Ibanez cry. She looked to the side of the stage; Sonia, Naomi, Maddie, and even Raine shouted encouragement, and Jeffrey, now one of *Kickback*'s roadies, stood devastatingly handsome in his uniform of band vest and shorts. He raised his right thumb in her direction.

"Go girl!"

It was time to shine. She might never get another chance; it *was* a farewell tour after all. Cindy awaited her cue, then stepped up to the microphone and let her voice ring out to the rafters.

THE END

FAREWELL

www.ingramcontent.com/pod-product-compliance
Lightning Source LLC
Chambersburg PA
CBHW070630130626
46555CB00006B/2505